Captive

written and illustrated by

Blaine Turner

The Dollhouse Trilogy

Captive

Copyright © 2008

by

Blaine P. Turner

ISBN 978-0-578-00165-4

This little book is dedicated with love to
my daughter Krista.

~1~
A More Complexing Age

First of all if you haven't finished the book <u>Trapped</u> then silly you. Go back and complete it. Okay, if you don't *have* it, that's fine. You can still read this book, but if you don't understand everything, it's not my fault. Come to think of it, you might not get everything right away even if you *have* read <u>Trapped</u> – for some ideas take a lot of pondering to sort out. Like how is it that mice can talk and people can fall in love? Maybe you don't believe this is actually possible. Sometimes I wonder about it myself, but then have only to fall back on what I've seen with my very own eyes and heard with my very own ears. Yes, fiction may be stranger than fact, but it's often more truthful. Or at least more wholesome and satisfying – let's say "Godly" – which is the definition of truth in my book.

For instance, I must apologize for implying at the end of my last book that Mary and I were married. Oops, I thought I could justify it in the name of good fiction or get away with it because at that time I had no plans to write this next book. Mary and me? I suppose it was just fanciful thinking on my part because, as you well know, she's much too beautiful and sophisticated to fall for the likes of me. Yet in her own special mansion, she sang to me like she was the very definition of love, and played on the harpsichord like the notes were the children of her heart. So naturally I became captive by the grace, the green eyes and the saucy brown hair that swirled when in song and smelled of bubble bath. Can you understand that?

Do you remember when we tumbled out of the dollhouse clinging to each other? That's the romantic way I reminisce, you see, and that's when I first knew we were in love. Otherwise why would she have been so embarrassed? I felt her blushing in my own face and the memory of it marked my mind forever. I remember how she held my hand as we descended the stairs to meet Aunt Clara. I recall how she stood shyly half behind me when we greeted the stern lady. I could feel the nervousness of her hand on my waist when Aunt Clara gasped and covered her mouth at the sight of her.

"Mary? – Is that you? You're so young," she had cried with a puzzled, almost shocked expression. Straight away her bony hand whisked her from my side and into a seat at the kitchen table. "Look at you, you're starving. Here, start with a nice glass of warm milk." She hovered and fussed incessantly until our parents arrived to pick us up. Curiously, we were swiftly ushered from the house and shushed whenever we broached the subject of Mary. Alas, it was not days, but many years before I would have the opportunity to see my Mary again. The Mary of my dreams. Perhaps I would never see her again. But my big chance came in a dream I had one night. How real are dreams? Well this one seemed pretty real. In it my sister Katherine found a note half-sticking out a dollhouse window on Aunt Clara's mysterious third floor. The note, in elegant, tiny handwriting, spoke cryptically:

Willy, find me at Smary@ChâteauChic.com

Of course "dot com" meant nothing to us in 1959, a time well before the internet. Nevertheless I tucked it into my pants, for I knew very well who Willy and Smary were.

That tiny slip of paper in a dream would prove to be my greatest quest in life. I remained captive to it even after my family moved out of town and all hope of seeing Mary again had fled. Ensnared I was, you could say. Do you fall further into the pit of love with only the *memory* of someone to cling to? Can you be increasingly enslaved by an ever fainting recollection? Can a fleeting dream imprison? Well I do suppose so. And the note, which existed only in my mind, just served to strengthen this supposition as time blundered on.

Well, time lumbered right into the 21st Century, bringing with it my 50th birthday alone and my own personal age of computers. It also brought me a second obsession – e-mail. I can still feel blood rushing to my skin the first time I saw a dot com address! That very day I found myself crazed, nervously typing into cyberspace from that old and yellowing scrap still tucked away in my head:

```
Smary@Château ...
```

But I'm getting ahead of my story. Perhaps I was dreaming this too. You will have to be patient with me. I get carried away.

I hope my little book will soon answer all your questions, and many more besides, which I'm sure will come up as we go along. But maybe it won't and that's the way life is sometimes. Then again, maybe there's a further surprise in store for you.

Oh well, to start with, you can stop thinking that this book begins where <u>Trapped</u> left off. Actually it starts way, way before that, even before you were born I shouldn't wonder. Unless you're quite a bit older than your parents, which is clearly impossible even in make-believe. Or *is* it?

Hmmm. Are you ready to begin? If not, don't go on to the next page! But I dare you to do it, and I think you're the sort of person who would, no matter the risks.

~2~
A Barren Old Wart Lady

The wart lady sat down in her rocking chair. It was a slow, graceful motion until the last six inches or so. Then it was an inglorious collapse which would scoot the rockers an inch or two closer to the wall. Eventually her head would start bumping the wallpaper when she rocked, leaving a grease spot, so she'd grunt, laboriously rise, and scoot the chair forward a foot or two, then crumple back into it again. The scratched floorboards can recount the story to you much better than I, and to everyone who comes into the house.

This was her entire existence, the old wart lady, except for her four radio knobs, a lamp switch on a frayed cord and her tattered afghan.

Yes, these things and a small, wooden-handled bell on a side table. This bell brought all the comfort, security and assistance of the outside world. Actually it only brought Aunt Clara, but they were one and the same to the wart lady. My Aunt Clara. Actually it was my *Great* Aunt Clara, but she would never admit to that title.

Now you might think the appellation "wart lady" to be unkind, but believe me when I tell you I'm trying to cast her in the most favorable light possible. "Wart, wrinkle and pus lady" would probably be more apropos to this situation, but truly unkind. Yes, even her ear lobes had warts, and many could be seen hiding in her thin, crooked gray hair. Yet it was the big one half-inside her nose that most assaulted your senses. That one had even grown a wart of its own with a thick black hair emergent from it.

Of course you might say it's the insides that count. And that'd be right, but unfortunately in this case, disappointing, as you will presently see.

"Clara!" came the intruding croak again, punctuated by the relentless bell. "Clara! Where are the children going to sleep? I'm thirsty again."

"There are no children, dear," Clara replied, rushing in with a syrupy smile, but she knew in her heart that the lady didn't believe her.

"My children!" the lady ranted, "have you sent them away? Have you done something worse? Something horrible? Get me some water. Where are my children?"

Now Clara knew this to be nonsense, but the lady knew otherwise, and put on the usual suspicious stare with her stagnant gray-green eyes. Over the years "suspicious" gradually turned into "malicious," so Aunt Clara began to think seriously about putting the old wart lady into a home.

"Oh you wouldn't do that!" the wart lady had wailed, "Not to your own flesh and blood. They yell at you in the home. They pinch you if you don't move fast enough down the hall, or up the hall or wherever they fancy. They get soapy water in your eyes. They make you eat fish sticks. They stole my wedding ring!"

Clara had to agree, in part, about the ring. When the old lady was sick in a nursing facility someone had stolen her ring; but it was only a cheap chip mounted crudely in a low quality metal band. Hardly worth the fuss. Nevertheless to the wart lady it was her hope-diamond set in gold and meant everything precious.

In point of fact, and I'm sorry to tell you this –the wart lady became so abhorrent that she began to be treated badly. Treated badly for this one reason alone. Ugliness. So when the horrible treatment caused inward resentment in her, then outward aggression, the abuse only spiraled further out of control. Soon this heartlessness on the part of others drilled a deep and festering bitterness into the wart lady's own heart and she became entirely repulsive, both inside and out.

This was exactly why Clara decided *not* to put the lady into a home, but rather to stick her up on the third floor. It was no more work really, because the lady needed so much help living downstairs anyway. Clara fixed up a nice bed for her and carried her rocking chair and side table up there too. On a separate table with two chairs she placed a small microwave oven and all the fixings for a tea party. A tea party of one, of course because even Aunt Clara could scarcely endure the wart lady's company of late. Besides, with the wart lady safely upstairs Clara could put her out of mind for whole blocks of time. And Clara's mind certainly needed, and yes, *deserved* the rest. So we can't really blame her unduly for also tucking the wooden-handled bell into a bottom drawer of the roll top desk. Then, as an afterthought she brought a couple of old dollhouses up from the basement for the old lady to look at. Finally, and as a last act of kindness, Aunt Clara firmly locked the crystal knobbed door to ensure that the wart lady would not fall down the steep stairs leading from the third floor.

Now Clara was not a cruel woman. To be sure, she visited the third floor several times daily. But she could now spend most of her time more profitably repairing the damage the old wart lady had done to her stately home and to her precious state of mind.

~3~
Tea for Two

For several days the wart lady listened quietly to her radio and watched the occasional cloud pass behind the one small, round window in her room. The yellow gingham curtains complemented the green walls tastefully but the lady soon tired of her surroundings. With the absence of Aunt Clara she would cry out to the dollhouses or to the steamer trunk in the corner. They, of course remained cold and stoic to her plight, even when she used the strongest language she knew, "DRAT and TARNATION! Where are the children? I'm thirsty for something besides tea."

One morning, one of the four knobs came off her big radio. Unfortunately it was the on/off switch, so there could be no radio that morning. The old wart lady stared blankly into space then slowly bowed her head into her lap and a single tear dropped sadly off her long nose and onto the wrinkled and gnarled hands folded below. Eventually the lady made herself a cup of tea and the steam from it was immediately soothing. As the lady rocked slowly back and forth, cup in hand, she caught a disturbing sight in the corner of one eye. More than disturbing, I should think, to an old lady. She was certain she had spied a mouse skirting about among the dollhouses.

A mouse so ugly that – but wait a minute. She knew all mice were ugly, malicious, and dragged disgusting tails behind them, but after it reappeared a few times she began to wonder if this particular mouse might be cuter than most. Like the ones you see on greeting cards (or in books like this one). At least it did seem presentable – tail and all.

"I must be exceedingly lonely to fancy a mouse," she mused whenever it scurried under the big door and presumably down the steps. Soon she found herself actually yearning for its return.

And return it always did. One time it even scaled the leg of the side table to gaze at her from beside the spare tea cup.

"Aren't you going to pour me some tea?" it said.

The lady almost fell over backward. She just stared at it with her eyes popping out almost as much as the mouse's. She was afraid to get out of her chair, afraid even to rock forward, for to do so would lean her closer to the mouse and its overly inquisitive whiskers.

Finally the mouse cocked its head and said, "I know you can talk because I've heard you moaning and groaning about everything under the sun for nigh on to a week now."

The wart lady hesitated and then said simply, "I didn't know you were thirsty."

"Mice are always thirsty in attics," came the reply.

"I'm sorry," said the lady, "can you manage if I pour a little into the saucer here?"

"Oh, I can drink from a cup, but not without indelicate posturing. But thank you, the saucer will be fine, however impolite."

"How is it that you can talk?" asked the lady.

"How is it that you are listening?" returned the mouse.

"I'm listening because there are no people to talk to here," said the lady.

The mouse wagged its head. "Oh, what about mice? Mice are most certainly people and of the best kind – only not *human* people."

"I'm sorry, I didn't know," said the lady. "Then why are you up here in the attic like me?"

"Well actually I'm moving into my same house."

"What?"

"I'm moving into the house I've always lived in."

"That's silly, you can't do that," said the lady, "unless you're playing make-believe."

"Yes I can, I'm not make-believing," said the mouse. "You see, the house itself was rudely and without proper notice moved up here from the basement and I just found it and am moving back in."

"Oh, I see," said the lady, turning her head. "Which house is it? That castle?"

The mouse threw up its front paws (which is hardly a grand gesture in rodents). "Dratl ratl scranlfritz!" it said, "not the castle. The nice big proper house nearly. Mousumerset Manor."

"Oh it has a name," said the lady, "and what a mouthful of name it is. Why don't you just call it Mouse-nest?"

"Why that's entirely too undignified for such an imposing edifice," said the mouse. "All noble houses should have a grandiose name, as befits their regal occupants."

This almost made the old lady chuckle but she thought better of it. "Then do *you* have a name, you smarty little mouse? Or should I just call you Minnie Mousie."

"Oh please don't!" said the mouse, genuinely disturbed. "I have a perfectly good name given to me by my mother-mouse. It is Luucy. We come from a long line of regal and beautiful personages."

"Do you find me regal and beautiful?" said the wart lady evenly, striking a pose.

"You are as beautiful as humans can aspire to be, I suppose," said Luucy, "but you lack the royal bearing and refinement of a true monarch. Besides you're a bit short on facial hair."

"But I'm *not* beautiful!" protested the lady. "See, I've lost my front tooth and the second is *this* loose. Look."

"Be careful!" cried Luucy, "Oh now look, you've pulled the other one out. How *ever* will you eat corn off the cob?"

"I don't like corn on the cob."

"Of course you don't. What good is corn *on* the cob?" said Luucy. "Only elephants eat that. Its corn *off* the cob which is fit to eat. And now you lack the teeth to get it off."

The old lady just smiled and asked what "dratl ratl scranlfritz" meant. Luucy replied that nobody remembered what it meant and that they'd never even heard it explained by the castle rats, and they were notorious for knowing *all* the words in the dictionary, and many that aren't. The mouse then enquired after the meaning of "DRAT and TARNATION" but the old lady didn't know that either.

The lady and her new mouse friend sat together through the whole pot of tea and then Luucy, noting the lateness of the hour, excused herself politely with a smile. Her mousy attempt at a grin made the lady giggle out loud and this stopped Luucy in all four of her tracks.

"I don't laugh at you, if you please," said the mouse, "what is your name anyway? Or should I just call you Minnie Mole-hill?" Luucy knew at once from the lady's expression that she had spoken unkindly.

"Oh, I'm sorry to make you cry," she said. "Please forgive me. I'm only a loud mouth mouse, you know. Please bid me farewell with one of your wonderful human smiles. I would be so grateful. Please. Pleasy please with powdered sugar on top."

Finally the old wart lady relented and broke down into her first truly warm-hearted smile in years.

"Thank you," said Luucy, "and by the way, by what name should I address you when I return?"

"Oh pleasy do come back soon," said the lady, "and when you do, you may call me your newest friend, Mary."

~4~
The Chamber Pot

The next day, Mary was using the chamber pot when Luucy walked in.

"I'll just be a minute, please excuse me," said Mary.

"For what?" said Luucy.

"Please excuse me while I finish going to the bathroom."

"You are excused. But you're *not* going anywhere, and certainly not to any bathroom. You're sitting on that funny stool, urinating in that pot. *Why*, I haven't the faintest idea. Do you have a special use for urine, that you're collecting it so carefully? We mice just get rid of it directly as soon as possible. We don't like it. We don't try to keep it around for who knows what purpose. What are you keeping it for? You don't put it in my tea do you?"

"*Excuse me* while I finish," replied Mary. When the mouse kept staring, she said, "I mean excuse *you*!"

"Whatever for? I've done nothing but stand here waiting for you," said Luucy.

"This is a chamber pot," said Mary, "Clara will come fetch it away soon. All I'm saying is that it's not polite to stare at someone on the pot."

"Oh I *see*," said Luucy, somewhat embarrassed, "I'll just wait over here by my doorstep. Will you be finished soon?"

"That's not polite to ask either!" said Mary.

"Oh I'm sorry," Luucy called from the corner of the room. "Come to think about it, I've heard how touchy humans are about anything that happens in the bathroom. I've also heard they carry nasal mucus around in fancy little cloths they keep warm next to their bodies. Whatever for? Is that an urban legend or is it for real? Do *you* do that, Mary?"

"Your house would be much cleaner if you used chamber pots," said Mary, ignoring the question, "But can we change the subject?"

"You've never been *in* my house, to remark so about its tidiness," said Luucy.

"Of course not, I'm not three inches tall."

"Well, when you're finished with your unmentionables, please come over here and have a look in my window. You'll see what gracious living really is." Luucy said this with perhaps a bit too much pride in her voice.

So when Mary was finished she did hobble over to the dollhouse where Luucy stood smartly by the heavy front door with its polished brass knocker. It was mounted in the center of the door and consisted of a hand holding a round ball. If you moved the hand up and down it would knock on the door.

Luucy noticed Mary's fascination with it and said, "It's from Spain. And the door itself is French. The hinges are from Germany, but the screws in them are only from Ace Hardware.

Would you like to come inside?"

"Don't be silly," said Mary. "Does the back of the dollhouse come off?"

"Oh no," said Luucy, "but we have a bat living in here that says you can fit into this house, if you try."

"How childish!" said Mary, "what would a bat know anyway."

"Bats are really intelligent," replied Luucy, "at least this one is. They're actually mice that have been to flight school. When they graduate they're given their wings."

Mary laughed and tried to kneel down to the house, but only succeeded in crumpling on the floor next to it, a pile of creaking bones. She rolled her head toward the mansion but her bony hand would not fit into any of the many doors or windows. "I guess I'll have to come in to see you another day," she said, mostly to humor the mouse. But part of her really *did* want to go in, because inside was the most splendid array of elegant furnishings she had ever seen, the most tantalizing of which was a great big claw-footed bathtub.

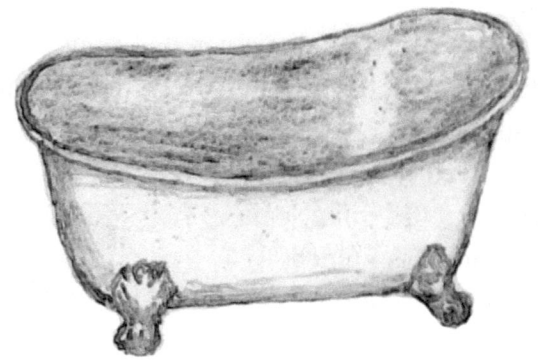

~5~
Mary Gets In

Many days passed and Mary thought she might be losing her mind. She began forgetting things, like how much sugar to put in a cup of tea, or which knob on the radio would change the station. The visits from Luucy helped, but eventually she began forgetting the many things Luucy had told her. Mary was distressed at being so rude and sometimes would say, "Oh Luucy, I'm sorry, I've forgotten your husband's name again," or "Oh Luucy, I'm sorry, have I told you that story before?" or just "Oh Luucy, I'm so sorry..." For Mary had even forgotten what she had forgotten about.

One rainy morning Luucy announced that this would be the day for Mary to have a cheer-up breakfast at Mousumerset Manor. "There is nothing quite like it," she said. "There are sweet rolls and jams, jellies; butters, margarine, or suet; various bird eggs every way imaginable; sausage in links or patties; and fresh milk from your choice of animal in any percentage fat you fancy. That's not to mention the great assortment of cheeses, curds and wheys; and coffees from every civilized country on the globe."

"Oh it sounds delightful, but I can't get in; I'm too old. And too ugly for such a splendid table," wept Mary.

"Come anyway," invited Luucy holding out a tiny paw, "you're not as old as you think, and, in my most discerning mouse-eyes, you are a most beautiful creature, and my best friend. Please don't dishonor me by claiming otherwise and by refusing my hospitality. Besides the bat and even his mother said you would be most welcome at Mousumerset Manor. So please come Mary."

After such a passionate speech Mary began to weep in earnest. She could hardly refuse so warm an invitation. So, clutching to the last childlike figments of her mind, and clinging to the last strength in her brittle bones, she crawled over to the dollhouse and tapped gently with the tiny knocker.

"Oh you don't need to knock," said Luucy, "you're family. Just go right in."

Mary must have forgotten that this was impossible, because that is exactly what she did. The impossible. She went *right in*.

Suddenly and terrifyingly Luucy became very big. As big as Mary. No wait. Of course, it was Mary who had shrunk – to Luucy's size. Mary was now a mere three inches tall. And it didn't hurt at all. The first thing she noticed about having such a small body, was that she was much more agile and nimble and quick. She began darting about the parlor like a moth.

"Mary, you'll wear yourself out or knock over a lamp," chided Luucy. "Come over here into the dining room. Would you like Earl Grey or English Breakfast Tea?"

The breakfast set before them was all that Luucy had promised, and then some. Even the table centerpiece consisted entirely of homemade breads, biscuits, buns and sweet rolls. Potato chips, breadsticks and tortillas were artfully arranged to resemble flowers.

"Tea?" Luucy repeated.

"Well, I'd really prefer to start with a giant glass of freshly squeezed orange juice," countered Mary. "If you please."

"Mary!" exclaimed Luucy, "be reasonable. All things in moderation, remember. We don't want to be ostentatious in front of the ants. Particularly with our everyday meals. Especially when there are so many starving children in China. Besides, the budget is tight and oranges don't grow on trees, you know.

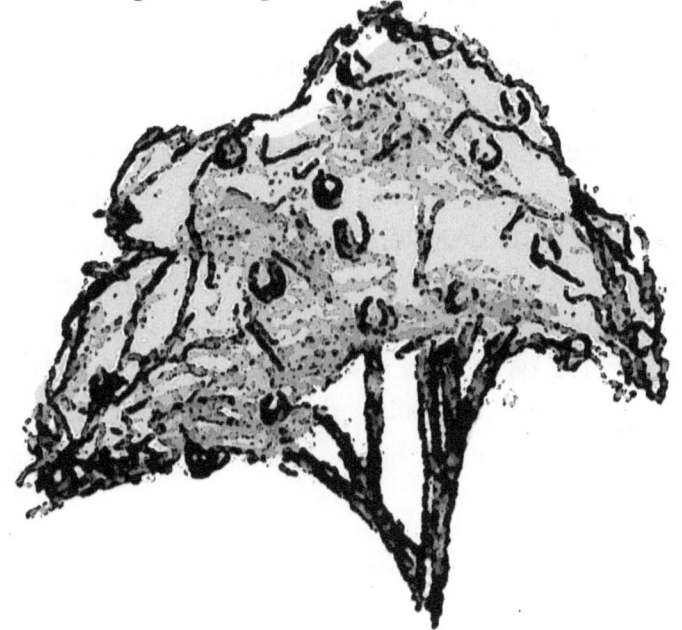

~6~
Adeylia Is Born

Over the next week or so Mary spent most of her time in Luucy's house, being very careful to scurry back to her chair whenever she heard Aunt Clara's key in the lock. All this growing and shrinking seemed to have no ill effects on her whatsoever. Fortunately for Mary, it was a very old lock and took quite a bit of fiddling before the door could be opened. Aunt Clara noted a new sparkle in Mary's eye and a blush in her cheek, but just attributed it to the peace and quiet afforded by the attic.

One day, Tuesday to be exact, Aunt Clara left breakfast *and* lunch, the latter encased in plastic wrap. She would be all day shopping and told Mary not to worry if she were late coming home. Mary just nodded dumbly but her mind was already buzzing with thoughts of Mousumerset Manor. For this was the very day that Luucy was due to have her baby! Or babies, rather, for mice have five or at least six at a time – to save on medical expenses. This also makes for much more profitable baby showers.

In fact, when Mary got to the manor the house was all abuzz with preparations for the big shower event. Luucy had registered herself with all the best stores so she wouldn't get duplicate gifts. How many baby bassinettes does one need anyway? Five or six mouse babies can easily fit into one bassinette, and one receiving blanket, for that matter.

Luucy showed Mary the litter shower checklist:

Timeline for hostess: [1]

Step 1: 6-8 weeks before shower

-Decide on the date and time with the Mother-to-be, and which future litter is to be honored.

-Prepare a guest list with Mother-to-be (no rats to be invited—some usually come anyway).

-Reserve restaurant or decide on a shower location. Avoid houses with cats.

-Decide on shower theme with Mother-to-be.

-Make or order invitations. One per household is sufficient.

-Make a list of food and beverages to be served.

Step 2: Since litters are often only 5-6 weeks apart, begin party preparations at step 1 at this time for the *next* litter. But be sure to keep on planning for *this* one.

Step 3: 4-6 weeks before shower

-Send out invitations.

-Keep a record of all names and addresses to give to the Mother-to-be to send out Thank You cards.

-Decide on what games will be played and what prizes will be awarded to the winners.

-Purchase prizes for game winners. Make sure you don't win all the prizes yourself.

-Begin shopping for litter shower favors. What is a favor? A favor is an item you give to each guest "thanking" them for coming to the shower. This is becoming more and more popular. A small piece of cheese will do! Do not give favors to rats, it only encourages them.

-Order decorations and party supplies that go with the theme. It's best if everything is edible, or at least disposable.

-Don't forget about the table centerpieces, this can be a gift for the new mommy or a game winner idea or even favors to pass out to guests. Try to get a 'usable' centerpiece so it can be used double purpose and saves money in the long run.

-For couples showers, don't forget about the new daddy! If you know who the daddy is, make certain he won't molest any of your guests.

-If siblings are going to attend, a small gift for them should be purchased. An extra piece of cheese is fine.

Step 4: 3 weeks from the litter shower

-Purchase and wrap your gift.

-Make sure that there are sufficient utensils and serving spoons.

-To avoid squabbles, make sure you have enough tables and chairs for the number of guests.

-Confirm reservations if the shower is held at a restaurant, spa or club.

-Order or make plans for the cake.

Step 5: 1 week before the shower

-Call guests that have not RSVP'd to see if they are coming. If they can't make it, send someone to pick up their gift. By the way,

RSVP stands for Reply So Very Politely.

-Clean your home and take a bath yourself (optional in some circles).

-In cold climates, prepare dishes that can be frozen.

-Arrange transportation for the Mom-to-Be.

-Arrange for someone to record names and gifts given, to give to the Mom-to-be for Thank You cards.

-Arrange for someone to hand the Mom-to-be the gifts, take the wrapping paper and place gifts to the side so everyone can see her opening the next one.

-Write out a timeline that you can follow to keep things on schedule such as play game number one, eat lunch, open gifts, play game 2, have dessert etc.

Step 6: 2 days before the shower

-Call the Mom-to-be about any last minute details. Arrange for babysitting for her present litter.

-Decorate for the party

-Set up tables and chairs. Always have some rat-sized folding chairs tucked away, should they be needed.

-Set up a gift table.

-Call bakery if cake has been ordered and confirm details.

Step 7: 1 day before the shower

-Make the remaining food on your list.

-If he is invited, remind the daddy of the party.

-Spot clean your home and trim your whiskers.

-Pick up flowers or centerpieces.

-Place several garbage receptacles in key areas so guests don't leave plates, napkins and trash on the tables to annoy the ants.

Step 8: The day of the party before guests arrive

-Relax, take a deep breath, but don't faint.

-Purchase or have balloons filled.

-Pick up the cake.

-Set up food and beverage tables.

Step 9: As the guests begin to arrive

-Greet each guest at the door, have them wipe their feet, and let them know where the refreshments are.

-To minimize fighting, introduce guests to one another.

-Have a comfortable chair, pillow and footstool ready for the Mother-to-be.

-Introduce the activities as they begin, explain the rules for games, announce when the meal or gift opening begins.

-When the party is over, have someone politely yell "cat" or "snake" and open the door wide so all guests can leave in an orderly fashion.

"My, my this seems like such a frightful lot of work," said Mary, glancing up from the list. "How do you keep up with it all?"

"Oh that's why mice always look so busy," said Luucy. "But parties are who we *are*, and parties we must have! Actually it's the multitude of mouse-weddings that keep us most busy nowadays, what with today's lapses in proper moral behavior. Nowadays there are certainly far more weddings than funerals, anyway. To my mind everyone should be limited to only one of each. That would be to El's liking too, I suppose."

"Who is El?" asked Mary.

"Oh, don't you know El?" gasped Luucy, "He's the Mighty One who made us all. Even humans. Even rats."

"You mean God?" said Mary, "sure, I believe in God, but I wouldn't presume to say I know him personally. I like to think of him as the man upstairs."

"Upstairs?" said Luucy. "Here we have only a bat upstairs and *he* certainly is not God. His mother told me that in the strictest confidence. But El is very real to all us creatures and we know Him personally."

Mary said she would have to think about this because human people would naturally have deeper relationships with God than rodents. Or at least they *should* have. She reflected on her past life but nothing happened. She couldn't really remember anything at all about herself. Had she had a relationship with God? Had she had children? Had she been married? Was he gorgeous, or just passably handsome? Was she pretty? Was she a dish? Then it dawned on her. She must at least have had a boyfriend. *Everyone* must by at least thirty. And if she did, I mean *when* she did, then he must have rejected her. For she would never have rejected any sort of boyfriend at all, she was certain of that. So he must have abandoned her, and if so where was God in all this? *He* must have abandoned her as well. And God, at least, would always have a good reason for His actions. It was a depressing thought.

Then something else dawned on her. If she *had* had a husband, or even just a boyfriend, then she must have had children, because literally *everyone* was doing that. It had become a tradition, in or out of marriage. At least that's how it seemed to her. But that doesn't make it right, right? Still, if this were the case, then her children must also have forgotten her. Because where were they now? Why would they do that? What was *wrong* with her?

"Do you think I was ever young and pretty?" she asked Luucy, her eyes moistening.

"Was?" said Luucy, "you still are." Then after a pause she added faintly, "To me, you are."

"Maybe all of me is beautiful except these unsightly moles and warts and blackheads," said Mary. "Everything but my thin flabby arms, wrinkly skin, thinning gray hair, flagpole-like carcass and flat feet."

Luucy gave her an odd, inquisitive look, then the moment passed. Soon days turned into weeks and weeks into the day of the shower!

It went by uneventfully and entirely according to the best laid plans of mice and Mary. Actually with all the hullabaloo and falderal of the preparations, the party itself was somewhat of a letdown. Only two rats showed up and they soon departed when the potato chips ran out. This is why the cakes are customarily brought out quite late in the festivities. All the guests departed on time leaving a small mountain of gifts and IOUs. In mouse society, the latter items can be re-gifted without comment to another person's litter shower. One wonders if soon *all* gifts will be IOUs.

Not long after the shower the litter actually arrived. Today in fact. For Luucy, it was no big deal, something she could fit in between preparing breakfast and brunch. A far greater task was naming the pups, but since she had only six, that was easily accomplished. She explained to Mary that, as a young mouse, she was only up to the A-Ds. So the names were duly recorded, in order of birth, as:

Adam, Adrienne, Adolph, Adelaide, Addison, and the smallest, Adeylia.

The newborns were blind and furless. Also plump, pink and wart-less Mary noted. Luucy explained that fur would start to grow some three days later and then the eyes would open in one or two weeks.

Looking at them all huddled in a row next to Luucy, Mary felt sorry that she herself had never had children. Or at least any she could remember.

"Luucy," she said, "with so many children, do you ever forget any?"

"Oh I get names mixed-up something awful," replied Luucy, "but I never would forget a child of mine. They each have a distinct look, smell, and personality. Why do you ask?"

"Oh, I'm just sorry not to have children myself," said Mary. "Now I'm too old. And if I weren't too old I'd be too ugly."

"In mouse culture ugly doesn't matter," said Luucy, "it's the smell that guys go wild about."

"Oh we have that too," said Mary. "We call it perfume, but it's very expensive and seldom overcomes an ugly face or stick-like shape, especially in the old ladies who use it most profusely."

"Humans certainly are strange," said Luucy, "but there just might be a way out for you."

"What might that be?" asked Mary, but she was cut off by a small army-like invasion taking place down around her feet.

~7~
A Solution Presents Itself

The ants arrived as always, without knocking, to clean up after the party. Luucy could certainly do without their sarcastic remarks about the sloppy habits of mice, but as usual, she was entirely appreciative of their work. And they work for crumbs. Ants, not being content with being neat-freaks themselves, feel compelled to order the lives of everyone else as well.

While they were there, Luucy took the head ant aside and whispered something at the side of his head, since she didn't notice any ears to speak of.

"That's highly unusual, irregular, egregious and stupid," the head ant said, "but it would afford a unique experience for our surgeons. Of course, for a human you would have to engage the services of the anesthesiologists. Can you trust them with such a ticklish task? We don't even like to *talk* to them. We can't stand to even *look* at them."

"Oh, I will do that," promised Luucy, somewhat fool heartedly, because up till that time, no mouse had ever spoken to a spider.

Nevertheless, the next day she climbed warily up the back stairs to the room which the spiders called their "sparlor." The door had a panel broken out of its lower half, big enough for Luucy to squeeze through without knocking. She should have knocked.

"Sintruder! Sintruder! Surrender!" came the alarm and immediately sixteen black and bulbous bodies swung down from the ceiling on silk threads. "Speak or die," said the sergeant general.

"Oh please!" stammered Luucy, "I mean you no harm. Here, I have a nice rice cake for you."

"What's snice abouts s'rice cakes? S'it's disgustings. S'it's disgracefuls. Vomitous. Swedes prefer some tiny's bitesies of *yous*!"

Luucy's legs quaked, "Oh, I'm so sorry. Would you prefer a fly or a fat caterpillar?"

"Scaterpillars? Oh s'could yous! Yums. And fats, spleasy, greasy-splease?"

"I've come to ask a favor of your anesthesiologists?" said Luucy.

"Firsts the Scaterpillars!" came the reply in unison. "And fatses for suckings!"

"Okay, okay. Give me a minute." said Luucy, gagging and retreating down the stairs.

It took her all day to find three big, fat caterpillars outside in the garden. They were so fat they couldn't even speak. She wrapped them in a scrap of newspaper and tied the package neatly with a thread. Impulsively, she added a bow of bright red ribbon and a Christmas gift sticker which she inscribed:

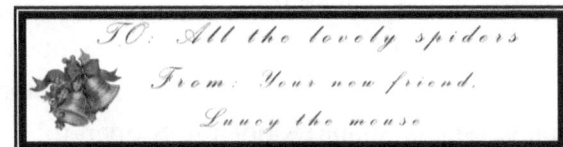

TO: All the lovely spiders
From: Your new friend.
Luucy the mouse

That evening she hastened back up the stairs and through the hole in the door. Mice have wonderful night vision and Luucy was actually relieved that she couldn't see things quite as starkly as in the daylight. It gave her just enough courage to complete her mission.

"Sintruder! Sintruder! Surrender!" came the alarm again and immediately the same sixteen black and bulbous bodies swung down from the ceiling on silk threads. "Speak or die," said the sergeant general.

"Oh please!" stammered Luucy, "I mean you no harm. I was just here. Here are the caterpillars you wanted."

At the word "caterpillar," the multitude of spiders began to descend all around Luucy. When they started up her ankles she threw the packet into the middle of the room, and they all scurried after it. Now spiders can bite through paper with their fangs, but they can't tear or cut it. They couldn't undo the thread either. After at least ten minutes of fruitless tussling and rude comments they turned on Luucy ominously and with one voice cried, "S'open it!"

Luucy thought to flee back out the hole but bravely stood her ground. "First promise you'll let me talk to your anesthesiologists, then I'll open your package."

There was some discussion and hissing, but finally a particularly large, but very wrinkly spider approached majestically on seven legs.

"I am Snana, and I promise. Now s'open it."

All the other spiders repeated in chorus, "She is Snana. She is Snana. S'open it. S'open it."

Luucy, assuming she was the queen or something, quickly approached the packet and deftly unwraped it with her razor-like teeth.

"Sthanks muchly," said Snana and she retreated to the feast.

Later, after all had had their fill (except Luucy who was quite nauseous by this time), seven spiders approached Luucy and cocked their heads. Since their heads are fused to their chests, this gesture gave them a menacing, robotic-like appearance. Their long fangs hung from the sides of their mouths like swords.

"Wells?" they said. "Wells, wells, wells?"

"Are you thirsty?" asked Luucy?

"Nottie thirstys. Wells, what do yous want with us'es?"

"Oh, are you the spider anesthesiologists?" asked Luucy.

"Not sanalologists," they said, "swee are's the ensleepers."

"So what's that?" asked Luucy.

"Swee puts things to sleep, so's to lay eggs in them for's happy tomorrows for the babies spiders."

"Could you put something to sleep, but not lay the eggs?" asked Luucy.

"Yessums maams. Snana has said so."

"Well, come then," coaxed Luucy, "see, I will show you the way. There are many dangers for cute little spiders. But I will protect you and I will show you safely home. Don't worry, mice never lie, at least not on purpose."

As they began descending the stairwell, Luucy peered over her shoulder and said, "Oh, come to think of it, I suppose only two of you will be needed. But thank you all."

Despite having five eyes each, the two remaining spiders had to hold on to Luucy's tail while descending the dark stairs. "What are your names?" asked the mouse in a somewhat quavering voice.

"We're's Shrosetta and Shalisha, but being twins, it will be hard for you to tell us'es apart."

"All spiders look alike to me," said Luucy.

"That's because you don't *know* any," said Shrosetta. "Shames on you. To know us'es is to love us'es."

"I'm sure that is so," said Luucy, swallowing hard. "Come, the operation is to take place over here in the kitchen where there's lots of water."

When Luucy and the spiders entered the room, all the ants scattered like ants, except for two soldiers with remarkably long legs, large jaws, and brave hearts. Their nick names were I-hop and J-walker. I don't have enough time to tell you their real names because ant names are notoriously long. In fact their names are much longer than the ants are themselves.

To diffuse the tension Luucy began speaking immediately, "Corporal Walker and Sergeant Hop, may I present Shrosetta and Shalisha."

"*General* Shrosetta," said Shrosetta, raising up on her hind legs.

"And *Admiral* Shalisha," said Shalisha, saluting.

"Admiral of *what,* stiff-head?" demanded I-hop.

"Admiral of my *kin*-ships," the spider replied, "and my *friend*-ships, swivel-head. Also admiral of *swordsman*-ship. By the way, where are the rest of your legs?"

"Here, here," interjected Luucy. "Be nice. We mustn't focus on our differences. El made us each unique according to our own kind and pursuant to His own purposes."

"El did. El did," said the spiders.

Luucy stared at the ants, but she knew that most ants are atheists, trusting not in El, but in their own complicated regulations and rules of law. Some people have said that the ant queen is their god, but most ants would deny it, preferring to put their trust in their own individual instincts and inclinations. Taken collectively, this amalgamation of similar minds becomes the purest form of democracy, yet a most trivial form of society.

"So lets get to work," said Luucy cheerily. "Bring in the patient."

Abigail, a daughter of Luucy by a former marriage, led Mary in by the hand and comforted her with a soft voice.

"Don't worry, sweet one," she said, "I'll be with you the whole time."

"Are you going to put me to sleep?" asked Mary?

"No, no," said Luucy, "this is no time for a nap. The spiders are going to numb your warts, one by one, and then the ants are going to cut them off with their sharp jaws. You won't feel a thing. And then afterwards your skin will be as smooth as a newborn mouse."

Ant I-hop glanced at her as if to say that it might not be as easy as that, but Shalisha was already expertly piercing a wart on Mary's arm. Soon just the right amount of poison was numbing the area without doing any permanent damage. At the correct time I-hop nimbly snipped off the wart and it rolled over the chair arm and on to the floor near J-walker. Absentmindedly he reached over to make a little snack of it but it was Luucy who pompously piped up.

"Spit that out, Corporal" she said, "remember your Surgeons' Code."

"What's the Surgeons' Code?" asked Mary, trying not to gaze at the area where the wart had been removed.

"Why, I have a copy of it right here on my kitchen wall," said Luucy. "If ants had pockets I'm sure they'd carry cards with the code in their wallets. If ants had wallets. Anyway, here it is on my kitchen wall for all to see."

Code of Surgeons

1. Ask questions first, cut later
2. Measure twice, cut once
3. Never cut and run
4. Don't take short cuts
5. One cut in time, saves nine
6. Never make cutting remarks
7. Never practice on live people
8. Don't eat anything you cut off
9. Sew up again anything you cut open
10. Relax, mistakes will grow back

"Did you notice commandment number eight?" said Luucy to Mary pointedly, but mostly for the benefit of Corporal J-walker. No one answered her. Everyone just went about their respective jobs: spiders numbing, ants cutting, Abigail calming Mary, and Luucy prattling on about points of procedure and progress.

Soon it came time to tackle Mary's face and the giant wart half inside her nose. Shrosetta was hesitant to go *inside* her nostril to get a good bite, prompting an impatient J-walker to give her just the tiniest little shove.

"Watch it buster," cried Shrosetta, "keep all your legs to yourself if you want to keep them."

"Sorry 'Setta,'" said J-walker, "I was afraid you were chickening out and there is nothing worse than a spineless spider."

"Look who's talking, you boneless boob," returned Shrosetta.

Again it was left to Luucy to play the peacemaker. "There, there, you two," she said. "Enough bickering. There's work to be done and I need to be thinking about making dinner. Do you have any idea how long it takes to cook everything by scratch? Do you even know how long it takes to cut up a carrot? I mean the proper way, making each slice into a little flower shape."

Of course again nobody was listening to her. They were too busy with the giant wart in the awkward position. Suddenly *snip* and there it went, big black hair and all, rolling down the front of Mary's dress and onto the floor. Only *this* time, out with it there came a great gush of blood which wouldn't stop flowing no matter how hard Luucy screamed at it or danced around the floor. Yelling at everyone in the room didn't help either. Soon everybody was running around in such a dither that Luucy had to excuse herself completely from the room, run down the hall and faint dead away on the fainting sofa.

It was Shalisha who saved the day by remembering point nine of the Surgeons' Code. Swiftly she jumped up on Mary's face and turning her abdomen to the bleeding nose, spun a tight, sticky bandage over the wound. Everything soon became calm again and the rest of the warts were removed without incident, and thankfully before Luucy awoke and returned.

"Oh my, you finished without me," she said when she did return. She seemed a little hurt, but Abigail distracted her with thoughts of cutting carrots for dinner.

Mary, for her part, had a long nap of recovery. In fact she slept for two days. But when she did awake she felt refreshed and free of any hint of warts or moles. In addition to that, and for the rest of her life she would have a new respect for ants and a special fondness for spiders. Little did she know however, that her relationship with the spider colony would soon be taking a very hairy turn indeed.

~8~
Make-up

"Wakeup, wakeup," called Luucy, "it's nearly noon and the sun has already been up twice."

Actually "called" is not a good choice of words because the mouse's snout was almost inside Mary's ear when she yelled. "Are you deaf? – Or dead?"

"Oh, *shut* it!," snapped Mary most impolitely.

When she fully awoke she apologized quite profusely and Luucy forgave her with as much flurry as she could muster.

"Halleluiah, your warts are gone!" chirped Luucy finally. "They are as if they never were, washed away as so many bird droppings on a white beach. Praise be to El."

When Mary reached for a hand mirror to confirm this, her heart rose because it was all true, and then fell because each wart had left behind an unsightly blemish. "Oh Luucy, what about all these hideous discolorations? I look like I have the measles!"

"Oh, you look fine, my dear," said Luucy, "You've had a hard life. People will understand. Just think of yourself as a spotted leopard or a ladybug."

"I don't *want* to be a ladybug!" wailed Mary. "I want to be a lovely young woman, with a husband and many children. Just like you."

"Of course you do," consoled Luucy. "But you're not a mouse. Yet I think I know just the thing we need!"

"What?" asked Mary.

"Product!" exclaimed Luucy.

"Product? What's that?"

"Why product is the answer to all your dreams," said Luucy. "Of course, it refers to a great *host* of products all designed to improve the appearance. Product – called make-up. Make-up can 'make up' for all the faults in a human face. It's not your fault you're a woman. Product makes up for this by emphasizing good features, while making defects, like your big nose less noticeable. Mice, of course all have proper size noses."

"Really?" asked Mary, "how can make-up hide my big nose?"

"Contour make-up, my dear," said Luucy. "Use highlight to straighten a crooked nose, or lengthen a short nose, or make a wide nose like yours thinner. Of course keep highlight off bumps or hooks. Then put a little shadow along the sides of the nose. But really Mary, with you we should start way at the beginning. Hmmm, let's see. What is your basic face shape?"

"I didn't know that faces had shapes," said Mary.

"Oh my, yes," said Luucy, "that is painfully obvious. Your face is too square and we must work with blush to create the illusion of length and offset the squareness in the jaw line."

"That won't hurt, will it?" asked Mary.

"Not unless you struggle," replied Luucy, "it's only powder really – mostly brushed off butterfly wings. But we don't want to get it into your eyes. Now rodents, having perfect inverted-triangle faces and proper facial hair, do not need such glamour products, although one occasionally sees a overly-mascarad rat mama. Disgusting."

So Luucy, now totally focused on the task at hand, had Mary lay back in a wicker chair near the sink and brushed a few wispy strands of thin gray hair off her forehead. Then with a wash cloth she cleaned her face thoroughly. Yes, the discoloration marks would be a problem but Luucy would try not to offend Mary with any unkind remarks about them. What good would that do? Luucy always prided herself in her diplomatic ways and impeccable good taste. She would never purposefully hurt anyone's feelings.

Next came the moisturizer layer which oddly enough came in three different jars. One she applied to the forehead and she mixed the other two together for the rest of the face.

"You see, Mary," said Luucy, "you have a combination of oily and dry skin. Your t-area is oily and your cheek and throat areas are dry. So I mix honey, lime juice and crushed almonds for the dry areas. For the oily skin I replace the lime juice with heavy whipping cream. Or is it the other way around? Oh well, when I get confused like this I just swab the whole face with oatmeal leftover from breakfast. Everything turns out fine.

"After a light wash I apply a thin layer of foundation, or in your case a somewhat thicker layer. Usually I accomplish this with a damp sponge, but dabbing on with a butter knife will be handy where those beauty spots of yours are.

"When the foundation layer is cured and set, it's time to apply the glamour stuff, the color. Eye shadow, blush, mascara. I'm getting excited already. You are going to be the most ravishing old lady in town. We finish it off with a light dusting of translucent powder."

"How do you know all this?" asked Mary.

"Are there no books? Are there no magazines?" replied Luucy. "And, as a professional, I follow a strict code of cosmeticians. Here, see I have it up on the wall right next to the surgeons code.

Code of Cosmeticians

1. Never stare at ugly people
2. Never laugh at anyone's make-up
3. Never smell anyone's perfume too closely
4. Use only as much foundation as necessary
5. Never charge extra for homely people
6. Never correlate head shape with intelligence
7. Enhance the patients natural assets, if any
8. Never mix mouse mousse with moose mousse

9. Lick off all brushes after each use

10. Always ask for your money before handing the patient a mirror

Afterwards Luucy led Mary upstairs to a nice soothing beauty bath. She half-filled the luxurious claw-footed tub with warm water, then tossed in one cup of powdered milk, one half cup of salt and one quarter cup of baby oil. Mary became so relaxed that she almost dozed off. Her eyes closed. The calming steam spiraled about her head and she breathed it in lovingly. It made her mascara run down her cheeks and a chunk of her foundation layer fell off into the tub. But so what. Mary cared not a bit – for to her, for that fleeting moment at least, she was the very image of loveliness.

~9~

The Lieutenant Commander

It was beautiful how the twelve ton airplane approached the one hundred thousand ton aircraft carrier. It was dusk and both were gray. Eerie lights shone from behind tiny windows and you could imagine small eyes peering out of all of them. The plane approached from behind the carrier, bent on alighting gracefully on the angled deck. But that surface was pitching twenty feet up and then twenty feet down with the waves. It was narrow, scarcely wider than the plane, especially when viewed one mile out on the landing path. True, there was an electronic glide path to follow and the fighter jet was a graceful bird on it. But the pilot, a man known notoriously as Jellyroll Jesse James, was needing all his skill and concentration just to keep the bird headed toward the nest.

You see, Jellyroll was upset with himself. It was his last mission before being considered for the rank of Commander and his landing had to be perfect, OK3. No big mistakes or marks on his record. No crashed planes, for instance.

Landing on a carrier deck is easily the most difficult thing a Navy pilot will ever attempt. Jellyroll had scores of successful ones chalked up to his credit, but each landing is a new one with challenges of its own. Today, for instance his mind was festering with the combat mission he had just completed. "What combat?" he said to himself. He had flown over Afghanistan for weeks and months now with never a skirmish, never anything exciting, never even an interesting cloud to look at. Combat indeed! Out of sheer boredom, he had slammed his F/A 18 Hornet into a vertical climb, and then dove straight down at a small mountain, avoiding it only at the last second. Alone over Kandahar, he thought he might as well have been over Kansas.

Then he had spotted an enemy camel that wouldn't be roaming around in Kansas. From the air it looked menacing – like a long-legged tank with a rocket launcher for a head. The surface-to-air missiles on its back looked like a camel's hump and it lumbered along purposefully as if seeking cover behind a huge rock. Suddenly a small, but unmistakable flash of light shot out from it and in one motion the pilot-warrior in him instinctively armed and fired an air-to-surface Maverick missile.

The missile had followed a curved path but hit the center of the target and virtually vaporized it. There was nothing left to see but smoke and dust. Nothing left of the nomad family's possessions tied to the camel. Nothing left of the shinny cooking pots, the rolled up blankets, or the two live chickens tied to the top. Nomads are known to strap their babies to camels as well, but like I said, there was nothing there to see. So who knows? Except perhaps the frantic people running around the huge rock wondering what sort of terror had just struck from the sky. And why.

Jellyroll had put his plane into a belly-roll and headed for home at Mach 1.5, nearly a thousand miles per hour. "One less dangerous camel in these parts is no loss," he thought to himself, but a small voice in his head kept niggling at him. Now it was interfering with his concentration on the landing.

Through his shiny visored helmet he could see the tiny orange light called the "meatball" emanating from the stern of the carrier. If he kept that positioned properly he would hit the deck perfectly and his tail hook would catch the third of four arresting wires.

The arresting wires are one-and-a-half-inch-thick steel cables which run about 3 inches above the deck at 40 foot intervals. They are attached on both ends to huge cylinders below deck which absorb the energy of the landing. The wires are pulled out to stop the aircraft.

Jellyroll kept the meatball in view and brought his airspeed down to just above stall speed. Then SMACK and JERK, he was on the deck. He throttled back immediately. He had hit full power in case all the wires were missed and he'd have to take off again. But the landing was perfect, OK3. He had snagged the third wire, which was the best. Fantastic, he thought. "I'm the greatest. No wave-off ever, for me. After all, I'm not known as Jellyroll Jesse James for nothing." Later that night in his bunk, however, his nagging heart came back at him and he felt mighty sorry for shooting that camel, even if it was only in sport.

Despite his perfect landing Jellyroll was passed over for promotion that month. "Excellent flyer, but too reckless," the official paper had stated. His commander had said, and I quote, "You're gunna get somebody killed one of these days." Unquote.

Jellyroll was fuming. "Whatdaya think war is for?" he whined to himself that evening. "What ever happened to the good ol' days of the cutlass, the dagger, and the devil-may-care?"

A few short months later, in port Jellyroll donned his best dress-white uniform, grabbed his last jelly sandwich from the galley, saluted the afterdeck and marched the rest of the way down the gangway. He carried no luggage, but his Navy sword was carefully tucked under his coat. He would never return to the ship again, and in fact it would be many years before I heard from my brother James again.

~10~
Silk Strands

Mary would have remained in the bath forever, had it not grown cold. So the mice bundled her up in a huge, hot hot-pink towel for a few minutes before dressing her. "It's so luxurious," thought Mary, "to have others dry you with a towel, but when oversize mice do it they're not always careful to avoid tickling you." Still, Mary did not complain.

"There now, let's look at you," said Luucy. "So clean and nice, and when we adjust your make-up you'll be the prettiest little girl in town."

Later that afternoon Mary inspected herself in the mirror and while satisfied in general, she did wonder if all this was just putting lipstick on a pig. And then there was her *hair*. It was the same old thin, gray, sparse was the word, angular and broken *straw*. That's it, she had *straw* for hair, straw which no manner of make-up could make up for. Indeed she considered herself still an old, ugly woman, and her mood declined rapidly.

Just then out of the blue, one of those big, black spiders called out to her from atop the door jam. "Smary," it said, "scum wis sme."

"What?" said Mary, not quite understanding the dialect.

"S'come with ssss'me."

"Why?" said Mary, now oddly gratified by the fact that she was not the ugliest creature in the room.

"Eye salve a surprises for yous."

"I'm not sure I'd want your surprises," said Mary. "But I don't want to be rude."

"Snot rude," said the spider, "Surprises sweet. You scum."

"Don't go with them," said Luucy, bursting into the room. "Rumor has it this group of spiders smothers people with thick cobwebs, sucks all their juices out, and then hangs the gruesome dried web masks about their room."

Mary frowned, hesitated but then decided to follow the black figure through the door anyway. She was always a sucker for surprises. She could certainly turn back, she said to herself, before it became too late. Soon, however, it *was* too late because the spider had led her up through a labyrinth of dark halls, passageways and steep stairwells. And she had followed like the proverbial fly.

"Swatch your said," it kept repeating in its thin, violin voice. "Don'st touchy the s'walls. Spider trails bees upon thems."

These spiders leave a network of almost invisible silk trails everywhere in the house. They call it the narrow way. Actually it's quite easy to follow, if you're a spider. A place without a proper silk trail leading to it can only invite trouble, they say. All baby spiders are taught that most destinations nowadays have no trail leading to them, although many spiders can be seen merrily heading that way. The foolish spiders call it the gusto way, but the wise call it the disgusto way.

"Where are we going?" asked Mary in a small voice.

"Swears you's'll finders keepers, sloozers sweepers. Sits varies sneer. Skeep sup wismi. Don'st guess lost."

The spider led Mary into a tiny room they called the "s'powder room." All along the walls were shelves with jars, bottles and containers which looked like fat saltshakers with large handles. The room had no windows but a fair bit of light could intrude from underneath the heavy door. The gap was big enough to let even the fattest spider slip under with ease. To get in, Mary of course had to open the door.

She did so to a chorus of "Disclose the store. Disclose the store. Slight certs the sighs. Sift you splease."

Mary tried to understand and be polite but her arms started shaking and she fumbled with the door handle.

"Sift you pleasy splease!" came the chorus again. "Bees skirt-eous at sleets."

"Yeh, yeh," said Mary, finally getting the door closed. A brief panic knotted her stomach until her eyes adjusted to the semi-darkness. "Odd," she thought, "to be comforted by the emerging vision of three score round, black spiders, each as large as my hand."

"Swell Smary, swellcomes sear."

Mary found this group of spiders harder to understand than the others. Their accent was thicker and their tone higher and more syrupy. Almost sticky like honey. Still, slowly she was able to tune her ear to their utterances and soon she was able to reply to them, after a fashion.

"What do you s'want with me? What's my surprise? Remember I have s'matches in my pocket, for secretly I smoke cigarettes."

"Smatches, cigarettes? Disgustings! What sever fours?" came the reply.

"Well, I could burn you. And then leave," said Mary.

"Spurn! Snow! How sawful! Yule snot, swill you?"

Mary was instantly ashamed of herself and tried to calm them down. "Of course I wouldn't s'burn you without just cause. Sigh love all the slittle spiders."

"El loves all the slittle spiders stew!" came the chorus. "S'red, yellowy, blacks sand white buoys! Babies stew."

Mary hung her head.

"Butts, don't sleeve," said the spiders.

"Of courses knot!" said Mary, feeling better.

"Then surprisey stymie!" said a tiny spider, springing up and down as if on eight pogo sticks.

"Yessie, yessie! S'tyme," they all chimed in.

Directly a particularly fat individual lumbered forward and addressed Mary in an oily voice. "Saire," she said simply.

S'air?" repeated Mary.

"Yessums, your saire."

"What about my hair?" asked Mary.

"Your slack of saire!" said the spider.

"Well I can't help that!" cried Mary.

54

"Weewee scan!" came the reply. Soon the whole room was singing. "Weewee scan! Weewee scan!"

"Can what?" asked Mary.

"Scan so snooze saire, weewee scan!"

"Sew new hair? You're kidding me," cried Mary.

"Snot skidding. Snot skidding. Thass swut swee stew!"

Mary chuckled at her new friends but decided to let them have their way. For an hour at most – then she'd have to be getting back. How she was going to accomplish that, she hadn't the foggiest.

"Standy sin the center of the scarpet," said the spiders, so Mary did just that.

Then from each corner of the room, a great silk thread descended, with its spinner firmly attached and working furiously with all its might and legs. Soon the four spiders were joined by four more, then eight, then sixteen, each spinning madly.

All this activity was not without accompanying discussion, deliberation and chitchat. When they talked among themselves the spiders spoke much faster and Mary could catch only the odd word here and there.

"Ssssss ssssss sssy sissy sassy," some said.

Others gasped and responded, "Ssss saucy sap."

"Saucy sap!" the first group responded, "Snot!"

To spare you, the reader from further torture with spider language, I will give you a free translation of the consensus reached. "A short neck, however pleasingly spider-like looks less so, and therefore more fitting for a human, if the hair is worn at ear level, or above. The higher the better. For less formal occasions we'll balance the cavernous nose by amassing hair at the back of the head with a blast of curls or a chignon. To soften the square, heavyset face, let's pile curvy waves and curls as high as practicality will permit. For the naturally pasty skin, we'll add pearls profusely in strands to the do, without, of course, becoming indecorous."

From the above you can see it was just as well that Mary was able to catch only the odd word or two.

Soon the thirty-two spiders above her head were spinning and climbing to and fro as if in some grand 3-D basketball game with sixteen on a side, fantastic rules, and square-dancing steps added in. Working from her neck up, the wigweavers, as they were called, securely attached anchoring strands to Mary's existing hair and then fashioned amazingly strong, but light and totally realistic hair curls, one built upon the other. The higher the hair do became, the more excited they became, and they probably would have worked until they reached the ceiling, had not a cry of "stop" come from the wigweaver leader.

After tucking in a few loose locks they draped several strands of beautiful pearls across the front of the hair in graceful arches. Now where would spiders on the third floor of a house, on the third floor of another house miles from the ocean, or even a fish market, get pearls you might ask. Well they made them, that's where. If you roll enough sticky silk tight together in a ball, viola, you get a pearl, with all the luster and better durability than the ones oysters make. And the neat thing is that it's completely natural, not manmade at all, which is *so* desirable nowadays. If you ask your local spiders, I'm sure they'll make you some. Many even have pearls to spare lying around their webs somewhere. And if you already have enough pearls for your own needs, they make unique gifts.

"Looky, looky in the smearor!" The spiders chirped excitedly in Mary's ear. She did just that, but at first had a hard time viewing all of herself at one time. Stepping back she could finally get a glimpse of the entirety, the enormity, the totality of her new hair. To say it was over-the-top would be an understatement. To say it was exquisite would be to demean it. To say it was dreamy might be to dream too much.

But upon complete reflection Mary had to admit it was an improvement over her previous hair situation.

Next the spiders dumped crushed talc all over it, being careful to first cover Mary's face with a cone of paper. Soon there was so much talcum powder flying about the room that even the spiders appeared quite white.

"Sits a dirty job, but someone sass to stew it,' they said.

The powder would absorb sweat and oils, thus keeping the wig clean, and lasting longer before a new wig would have to be woven. Even though they were completely waterproof, no one ever bothered to wash a spider wig, when weaving a new one was so little trouble.

"How did you spiders learn all this?" asked Mary.

"Scums naturally," came the reply. "Sand we stake stootering from sour sellders. Salsa we salve sour Scode of Swigs."

Sure enough, on the wall was their "Code of Wigweavers." It was in English because Spiderspeak is still an unwritten language, which is unfortunate because it is well known that more individuals speak Spiderspeak than English.

Code of Wigweavers
1. The best wigs are white
2. The best wigs don't fly off in the wind
3. Realistic wigs have dandruff
4. Practical wigs keep the head warm
5. Never make dry-clean-only wigs
6. Never take a wig to the barber shop
7. Never give a wig to a dog
8. Never call a wig a 'rug'
9. A lady's wig is her crowning glory
10. A man's wig is his last resort

Mary touched her wig here and there and was surprised it was not sticky.

"How come it's not sticky?" she asked of the weavers.

"Stickys sinside, snot soutside," came the reply.

Fact is, spider webs are not sticky everywhere, otherwise the spiders would get caught in their own webs themselves. This is true of people too, but we're not as smart as spiders. We often weave dangerous, sticky webs around our lives and then wonder why we get caught in them ourselves. How sad and truly pathetic we humans sometimes are. I'm thinking especially of my little brother James, who deserted a promising career in the Navy for an impossible dream. Totally stupid. Warped. Of course, in this book *nothing* is quite impossible, as we shall soon see.

~11~
Capture The Castle

All his adult life James had longed for his pirate life as a young boy. Even when he was flying fighters off carriers he missed the pure adventure of the tall ship and the cannon ball. As a boy his sword had had 'real' blood on it. As a man he only wore his sword to parties to impress the ladies. How utterly ludicrous, a deadly sword strapped to a lily-white dress uniform. All tinsel and no toil. And he never carried his sword into battle, only a steering wheel.

After James walked off the ship, he took a bus and then a taxi straight to his Aunt Clara's house where he knew he would get a hot meal and lots of sympathy. He could deal with his parents later, he thought. If necessary, that is. For you see, he was trying to run away from real life and that's a hard thing to do. And very dangerous. But danger was the very thing luring him in. The danger and the suspense of it all.

Aunt Clara beamed with pride when she opened her door to a marvelous looking James all decked out in the dress-white uniform of a Navy Lieutenant Commander.

60

"Oh James," she exclaimed, "you are so handsome, so dashing. Your brother William was just here and he's still only an assistant manager over at Frankie's Chicken. He has to wear a ridiculous looking hat. But look at *you*, a General! How long can you stay?"

"Only for dinner, really," said James, "then I'll have to leave tomorrow morning before you're even up. Don't worry, I'll let myself out. Special military business."

"Secret?" asked Aunt Clara.

"Top secret actually," said James, "but you needn't worry, its not dangerous. Are there any jelly donuts in the kitchen right now?"

"Well let's see if William left any for you. No, it doesn't look like he did. But that's just as well, you need good, wholesome Navy food where you're going."

"Yeah, right," said James, "in the Navy I eat mostly jellyrolls."

Aunt Clara laughed and began pulling down pots for making an elaborate dinner fit for a General.

"Actually, Generals are in the Army," said James, "the Navy has Admirals."

"Oh, I'm so sorry, Admiral," said Aunt Clara, "are you hungry?"

"Always!" said the 'Admiral,' cutting himself a piece of cheese.

After a quick meal of steak, mashed potatoes, peas, pie, iced tea, and plenty of rolls with butter and jelly, James retired to the guest room and pretended to go to sleep. It was just like he was a little boy again, and just like when he was a little boy, he climbed up the stairs to the third floor as soon as he heard snoring from Aunt Clara's room. This time however, he forgot that his sister Katherine had always kept the key to the door. Now where in the world would she have found it? He didn't have a clue, but what he did have was the ingenuity to pick the lock with a piece of wire that he found in his room. It was an old lock and quite easy to do. He didn't even soil his white uniform.

Once inside, James went straight to the castle and with his Navy sword strapped to his side, went straight in. Yes, *straight in*! None of that wishing or believing stuff that had confounded his brother and sister. He just went straight in, and of course, immediately became three inches high. Or four actually, because he was a tall man to start with.

"Levancrieff Castle," he yelled once inside the portcullis, "I challenge thee, I invade thee, I conquer thee. And command the release of all fair maidens into my immediate custody. Blonds first."

All this ruckus woke Prince Sherwoode, who hadn't aged a bit since his last encounter with James. "To arms," he said, "and legs! Go drive off this pompous pillager before I'm too awake to fall back to sleep. Try not to kill him or spill anything messy on the floor. Call me in the morning."

With this, the entire rat garrison mustered with every sword, saber, rapier, dagger, cutlass and kitchen knife in the castle. Everyone from rat Private Low Class, to rat Field Marshal Superior turned out. Even some rats who weren't even *in* the Army showed up just for the fun, because, after all, they were facing an enemy of just one.

Also, it had been such a long time since their last battle that their stories were growing stale, even when exaggerated.

It was somewhat of a miracle that James made it all the way to the Great Hall with his charge. It was probably due to the fact that the rats were so disorganized they kept bumping into each other and yelling "en garde" or "touché" all the time. Still, it was not long before the Army had James surrounded with hundreds of steel points pointed directly at his throat.

When James said he surrendered, the ranking rat present, a particularly fat Brigadier Sergeant yelled the command, "Company, Right Shoulder, Arms!" This usually restores order, but because rats don't have any shoulders to speak of, all the weapons simply fell to the floor. In the ensuing melee James was able to slip away and up to the very chambers of Prince Sherwoode.

"Hey Woodiekins," said James, poking him with the point of his sword. "Look, I'm all grown up now. I just conquered your castle, by the way."

"Oh James, I remember you," said Sherwoode, brushing the sword away. "From the book Trapped. You're the one who will hide behind your sister's skirt."

"I most certainly will *not*," protested James, "besides, it doesn't matter now. I have you beaten and demand your sword in surrender."

"Oh, is that all?" said Sherwoode. "Go ahead, you can have any of those stashed away in the corner."

"No," replied James, "I demand your personal sword of power, your precious treasure, nothing less than the greatsword Logokrataioo."

"You stupid boy," said Sherwoode, "don't you know that Logokrataioo will be stolen from us by your noxious but brave big sister, so you can't have it now. Tell her she should have given it back right away! It wouldn't have been too much trouble for her. It wouldn't have been too inconvenient. It wouldn't have taken her too far out of her way."

While the Prince was talking, the rat garrison had regrouped, crept up the stairs silently, and now succeeded in getting the drop on James again, this time from the back. This time it was the prince who gave the orders.

"Because of his treachery, I order you to remove this foul person, however well dressed, from my presence and from this castle. You may return his sword to him outside the gate, but don't give him any cake or jelly, not one morsel."

The rats mocked James all the way down and even threw him in the green mud of the moat surrounding Levancrieff.

"There, sail in the mud, sailor," they called. "And use your Navy sword as a paddle," they said, spearing his sword deep into the muck beside him.

James, grown man though he was, started to cry. He decided it was no fun being on the losing side and that bravery in defeat is the height of foolishness. He decided he must *win* all his future battles and, to do so, he must choose them carefully. Surely, he thought, the best place to win battles would be in that hoity-toity white mansion next door. Why, he could make short work of it. And inside, there would be jellyrolls and mashed potatoes aplenty to plunder. Oh, what havoc he would create.

~12~
In The Mansion Instead

Will he meet Mary? Well I can answer that right away. No. And yes. In other words: Not yet. Read on, you'll see what I mean.

Early next morning James, sword in hand, and clothes washed and dried in the basement machines, headed for the stately old manor house and walked right in without so much as a knock.

"Wipe your feet," said a mouse butler, "if you please. And state your business."

"I demand to see the old bat," said James, returning his sword to its scabbard.

"In this house you don't *demand* anything," said Luucy, emerging from the sitting room door. "A polite request with a 'please' attached will do fine. For starters. What's more, have the common decency to lower your voice to a civilized level of conversation. Everyone in the house is still sleeping."

"Well then," huffed James, "I demand to *please* see the bat named Ivanhoe, for he will know where I can seek my treasure and find my pleasure."

When Luucy didn't say anything, James added, "*If you please*. And I'll thank you for the courtesy of a reply – TODAY."

"Courtesy is as courtesy does," replied Luucy with a curtsy.

"Enough statements, show me the stairs!" said James.

"The stairs will find themselves," said Luucy, "just look up."

With this, James walked out of the room in a huff. He did find many sets of stairs and figured by always taking those that went up, he'd eventually get to the bat. He found wide staircases, narrow staircases, spiral staircases, secret staircases, and even one staircase leading nowhere. But he had figured wrong. He came out not in the bat's room, but on the roof, on the widow's walk to be exact. You could see for miles, except of course this was only a dollhouse so you could see only as far as the far wall. James reflected on the meaning of the widow's walk. The handsome, dashing prince rescues the beautiful maiden from the dragon's disgusting lair. He then installs her in an imposing mansion and dashes off to fight other battles. That's what he does for a living, after all. Then his luck runs out and he's killed. Valiantly in battle, of course. But nevertheless, his lady paces the ridgeline of her house in the vain hope of sighting the masts of his ship on the horizon. The widow's walk, a sad result of misguided male courage and bravery.

But James was not a widow and never intended to be. He was seeking the bat and as luck would have it, spied his window just across the sloping roof from the railing he was leaning over. It was no great chore for the agile James to leap, shinny and shuffle his way over and bound across the sill.

At this sudden and rude intrusion, the bat woke with a start, and started fluttering all about the room crying, "Chee, chee, chee." Some of us already know what that word means. The others can use their imaginations and they'd be essentially correct. James remained very still and when the bat finally alighted on his perch again it said, "Whoa, window enterer, who or what are you? Are you applying for the position of chauffer in that uniform. I'm sorry, I don't even *have* a car. What with the price of gas and maintenance now days, I prefer to fly. Did you know there are more accidents on the highways than in the air?"

"Never mind that," said James rudely, "I've come to seek my treasure, the adventure of my life, and the pleasure of my desire. Please tell me where I should go."

"Aren't you too old for all that?" asked the bat, "you look like you're pushing thirty-seven. Say, how did you get in here, anyway? You're an adult, surely. Albeit a very small one. Yes, how did you shrink if you're so mature?"

"I used my trusty sword of power, here. See. I could trim your whiskers with it as easy as cutting a jellyroll."

"Oh, I see," said the bat, "you're not so mature after all. In fact you're probably just the little boy let out in you to chase off the man. That makes you nothing but a contradiction, a conundrum, a discombobulation."

James looked confused, but said simply, "Help me find my adventure!"

"You can't find the adventure you seek as a boyish man. It will elude you forever. Frustrate you. Laugh at you. And you will only become a failure. No, you must find this kind of adventure as a manly boy. You must become a real child again, but not a pussycat. You must become a boy with the heart of a lion, the legs of a cheetah, the stealth of a jaguar, the cunning of a puma. Other boys must call you 'saber-tooth,' and the girls must call you 'tiger.' In short, you must go back and grow up, before becoming a man."

"How can I go back and be a boy?" asked James, "do you have a time machine, or something?"

"You don't need a time machine to manipulate time," said the bat. "You see, ours are not just lives which pass through time, but rather it is time which, for a season passes through our lives. El lives outside of time and adjusts and re-adjusts it at will. So there are many ways for you to become a real boy."

"Okay, bat-brain," said James, "sounds fun, but as ridiculous as, well, this whole dollhouse scene."

Then it hit him. Here he was a four inch high Naval Officer stating that a bat had just said something ridiculous. He threw up his hands. "Okay, I give in, where do I sign up?"

"For what?" asked the bat.

"To become a boy again, find my adventure and grow up right."

"Oh you poor thing, we usually don't have the luxury of choosing a second boyhood. Unless –." The bat cocked his head at James.

"Unless what?"

"Well, there's always that French dollhouse over there in the corner."

"Fancy that," said James, glancing over into the corner, "a dollhouse within a dollhouse. Is that house magic too? What's in there? Can I go in it?"

"All your dreams are in there," said the bat, "but there's a catch. You become younger and younger, so it takes a lot of discipline to grow up and leave that place."

"Do they feed you in there?" asked James.

"You'll be a quarter inch tall," replied the bat, "how much would you need? A drop of honey and a cake crumb would last you a week. The ants could feed you from their leftovers."

"Can I take my sword and uniform in?" squealed James.

"Sure, but the house is full of swords and uniforms to try out. Some will surprise you."

"Is there any trick to getting in, like being childish or retarded or something? By the way, how did I get in here anyway, and if I grow up in here, will I get trapped? Can you explain the whole thing to me one more time?"

"Well the truth is," began the bat, "these dollhouses are only imperfect models of the true Kingdom of El. You see, dollhouses are only fantasies of our minds, but the Kingdom is real. You have to be childlike to get into both, but fantasy traps, while reality embraces. Beware the fantasy, but share the reality."

James didn't quite understand the bat, he never did, but he was eager and ready to enter the French house.

The place itself was imposing, L-shaped, four stories with a little, round tower in the center. That's where the frail, green-eyed maiden in the lace dress would be kept captive. Somehow the house looked like several smaller buildings put together haphazardly. It was very old-looking and worn with a yellowish tint to the stonework. There were many chimneys and too many weathervanes perched above mysterious attics. James had no trouble picturing the basements and dungeons that must lurk below ground. He was sure there would even be a hidden tunnel to a secret garden out back. And what would be buried out there? Well it made his heart quiver.

"I'm going in now," he said to the bat. And sword at the ready, he did just that.

He expected to be met by a uniformed security guard, or at least a butler. But no, as he careened through the door he was greeted by none other than an ordinary, common nine-spotted ladybug. Of course to him it looked like a Volkswagen Beetle.

"Hellllo, Laction-figure," said the bug, glancing at his sword. "I'm Marta. Wellcome to Château Fantastique. Lif you're here to rescue me, forget lit. Lie llive here and llove lit. Put that thing down, you'llll chip the woodwork. First loff, to what do we deserve the plleasure love your company?"

James just stood there, bewildered, "What?"

"Why lar you here, Stupid?"

"I, uh, well, I'm here to rescue the fair captive princess in the lace dress."

"How do you know there's la princess here?" demanded Marta.

"There's a princess in every household," said James.

"Wellll you're right labout that!" said the ladybug, inspecting her lipstick, "but you can't see her. She's lupstairs having la sick headache. And when *she's* not happy, *nobody's* happy. You woulldn't want to meet *her* lanyway. Lallways feeling poorly she liz, land throwing lup. Won't clean lit lup leither.

"What're you realllly here for? Lie bet lit's the jellllycake. My loan concoction. Lime known for lit lin these parts. A recipe for rapture. Lit'llll sllay you. You'llll be captivated by lit, consumed by lit. Laha, lie can see lit lin your lies. Wellcome then, for you've reached your finall destination, your finall resting pllace, your lultimate labode. Captive lin your very loan Château Gâteau."

Again, James just stood there stupidly.

"That means 'cake house' Dimwit," snapped the bug, "here, sit down, lie'll bring you la plate. But first remove that silllly sword, land that silllly smille. You'llll put your lye lout."

~13~
Inside Château Gâteau

Marta dutifully brought James his jellycake, and then she hovered over his every bite. "Now lizn't that just to die for?" she said, "but don't chew with your mouth lopen."

James had to admit that it was delicious, but didn't want to admit it to *her*. "Tolerable," he said.

"Tollerable? Cupcake, that's not what those sticky crumbs smeared lon your face say," she retorted, fluttering her wing covers. "They say terrific!"

James licked his lips.

"Wellll, lie suppose lit's time to show you the treasure room," she said. "Go wash those fillthy hands first."

"Stop telling me everything to do, ladybug!" said James.

"Llisten, Solldier-boy," fllashed Marta, "Lime not la lladybug, Lie should be properlly referred to laz la 'lladybird beetlle.' And la specimen love rare quallity, lat that."

"You're rare okay," mumbled James over his shoulder as she was marching him toward the bathroom.

So it was with properly clean hands (Marta had to send him back to comb his hair too), that they entered the enchanted realm of the treasure room.

James was immediately disappointed to find that the 'treasure' therein consisted of nothing but garments.

"Some treasure," he said, "it's like getting only clothes for Christmas and no toys."

Marta replied by pulling him by the hand through the racks and racks of coats, hats, shirts, pants, shoes and even underwear.

"Leeven Superman wore skivvies, Sweetie-pie," she said.

But James was already mesmerized by the Samurai battle uniforms and trying on a helmet for size.

"One size fits lall, Pretty-boy," said Marta, "try the whole thing lon. Have you lever worn more than one sword lat la time? Do you think you're coordinated lenough? Most men lie know can't walk land chew gum lat the same time."

"Oh, put a lid on it, bug," said James. "Why don't you just take a walk in the tulip garden or something?"

"We don't *have* la tullip garden, but lif we did, lime sure lit'd be your favorite pllace, Two-llips."

By this time, James had had it. He drew his magnificent Samurai sword and began scooting the ladybird out the door by the business end.

"Watch lit, Buster," she said, "don't get fresh with that stick. Lime getting lout. Give me la yell lif you need anything. Eye'll just be checking my leemail."

The château seemed too old to have email, but James let it drop in an effort to further the annoying bug out the door.

Not long after he was alone, and completely dressed in the Samurai uniform, James decided to search for the lace princess. The bug didn't speak well of her, but anyone that difficult must be very beautiful indeed. For plain girls just get smacked down in their places, but pretty ones can twist everyone around them to their own ends. "Watch out for the eye-catching ones," he always said to himself, but they were precisely the ones he was usually on the watch for.

There's a mouse legend, I don't know if it's true or not, that God's most beautiful creatures, bugs especially, will always climb *up*, while the uglier ones will always climb *down*, even burrowing into the dirt. The very prettiest, therefore can be found in the highest towers, some even being kept there against their will. Taken in, they are, by beasts or monsters captivated by their luring appeal. Captives of the captivated. Such a person must be this lace-girl, this damsel in distress.

However, after just one flight of stairs, all the cumbersome armor annoyed James. Yet rescuing a princess without every bit of it seemed besmirching of her honor. So it was a sweaty-faced figure who, after regaining his breath, prepared to knock at the tower attic door. Then it occurred to him that rescuers never knock, they simply bust the door down, on the first try mind you, burst in yelling, and immediately lock the villainous kidnapper in desperate hand-to-hand combat.

This James did, with all the bravado and braggadocio he could muster in his diminutive quarter-inch-high body.

"Hark and hellfire," he hailed, barging in and thrusting his sword wildly in the air at no one in particular. "You are hereby rescued, redeemed and recovered. Veni, vidi, vici!" which loosely translated means, 'I'm here, see, so deal with it.'

But instead of mortal combat, James found something even more dangerous, a princess in a bathtub.

"HOW DARE YOU!" she screamed from somewhere beneath a mountain of bubbles, "put that thing away before you knock over a lampshade. And wipe your feet. No wait. Just get out. Wipe your feet later, and then knock properly."

James was so caught off guard he did exactly as ordered and stumbled out. He even replaced the door crookedly back on its hinges. After a few minutes of wringing his hands, he politely knocked and called out in a manly, if breaking voice, "Okay, your huh-highness, are you ready to ruh-receive your Puh-Prince?"

"Oh no, you don't have an accent too, do you?"

"Of course not!" said James. "Only when I'm nervous. Can I just come in and rescue you?"

"I doubt if you *can* in that playsuit," said the princess, "try taking off half of it and see what happens. If you are handsome enough I will consider receiving you at the foot of my throne. Leave your hat and cape outside, mind you."

James felt humiliated. Not only was there no villain to slay, but the princess was turning out to be no better than the ladybug. Of course he hadn't had a chance to *see* her yet. She must be outstandingly gorgeous to speak so boldly. He stripped down to his tights and chainmail, then timidly tiptoed through the door again.

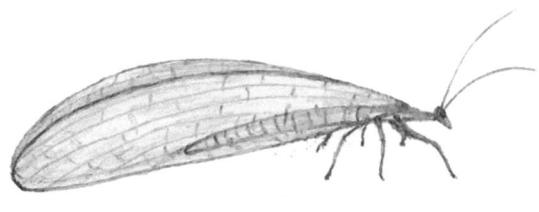 Her beauty was all that he could have imagined, and then an awful lot more. She was, in a word, breathtaking, and he had to concentrate on breathing. She was slim, graceful and fine featured. Her peignoir gown of intricate lace was shyly translucent but radiated a regal splendor. The antithesis of the ladybug, her big, black eyes greeted his warmly.

"Why are you here for me?" she asked simply.

"I – I didn't know you were an insect," he said.

"I am a lacewing," she said, "white, with just a tinge of green, and yes, you are a hue-man, white, with just a tinge of red."

James blushed. "I'm sorry to have frightened you in your bubble-bath."

"Not frightened, just, well disappointed that the first man to barge into this tower is only a hue-man, not a lace-man. Don't take it personal, though."

"I could find another costume downstairs," said James.

"Oh, that wouldn't help," she said. "It's the man that makes the clothes!"

James looked crestfallen.

"Oh, you poor thing," she said, "I've hurt you. I can see right through you. You need a damselfly in distress. Here, would you like to carry around a picture of me? Would that help?"

On the back she had already inscribed:

"What is your name, so I can fill

> To _ _ _ _ _ _ _ _ _ _ _ _
> Love from Her Grace
> the Lacewing Princess

in the blank?" she said.

"Aha," said James, "I can see right through you too. You're just waiting here in vain for your prince-man. Before you get old and shrivel up, that is. Is that it, your grace?"

The lovely lacewing immediately began to cry and then began to look sick.

"Oh please don't throw up," said James, "I didn't mean it. I speak before I think sometimes. I just know your prince wing-man is going to come through that door real soon."

"No, I'm too ugly."

"*What*? You ugly?"

"You don't know my past," said the princess, "I was fat, frumpy, and ate like a grub – a grub with a big nose and acne."

"I don't believe it."

"I have a picture to prove it, but you can't see it. No. No! Well, I hid it away at the end of this book, if you *insist* on taking a peek. But please don't laugh or show it to Marta, will you? And don't bring it back here to remind me."

"Marta was a grub in her youth," said James.

"Really?" said the princess through a thin smile, "she told me she was in baby beauty pageants."

"Only babies their mothers could love, I'm sure. Did your mother love you, your grace?" asked James.

"I never knew my mother," exclaimed the princess. It's like she just laid us kids down somewhere and then took off."

"Gee, how sad," said James, "how dysfunctional. Do you have a name other than 'your grace,' your grace?"

"Marta calls me Mayrie. She thinks she's a princess too, although who would know why!"

"Do you know El?"

"Who told you about El?"

"The bat," said James, "El would think of Marta as a princess, too, I'm sure."

"Then El is short on good taste and not very discriminating," said Mayrie. "I must say, Marta is more the domestic type, better at serving guests than receiving them. And she speaks with a 'laxcent.'"

80

"Yet he finds her beautiful. He finds *you* beautiful as well."

"Just like I said, his judgment is in serious question. I'm nothing but a worm in a silk dressing gown."

"Oh Mayrie," said James, "all of us have awkward child-hoods, but learn to live past them. Just look what you've become!"

"You don't think I'm spoiled?"

"Spoiled, why you're not even ripe yet."

"James, you're so clever, where do you get all your wisdom?"

"From the Samurai Creed I found in the jacket I left outside your door."

"Will you recite it to me?"

"Of course, it's no secret.

The Samurai Creed [2]

1 I have no parents; I make the Clouds and the Trees my parents.
2 I have no divine power; I make Truth my Divine Power.
3 I have no magic power; I make Wit my Magic Power.
4 I have no eyes; I make The Stars my eyes.
5 I have no ears; I make The Birds my Ears.
6 I have no laws; I make Self-Defense my Laws.
7 I have no strategy; I make the Right to Kill my Strategy.
8 I have no designs; I make Seizing the Opportunity my Designs.
9 I have no principles; I make Flexibility my Principle.
10 I have no friends; I make my Dreams my Friend.

Say, Mayrie, do you have a lacewing princess creed?"

"Well, no, but I do follow a Royal Insect Code.

The Royal Insect Code

1 I have no parents; I make El my parents.
2 I have no divine power; I make El my Divine Power.
3 I have no magic power; I make El my Magic Power.
4 I have no eyes; I make El my eyes.
5 I have no ears; I make El my Ears.
6 I have no laws; I make El's Laws my Laws.
7 I have no strategy; I make knowing El my Strategy.
8 I have no designs; I make loving El my Designs.
9 I have no principles; I make serving El my Principle.
10 I have no friends; I make my El my Friend."

"Mayrie, are you toying with me?" asked James.

"Oh, I sincerely hope so," she replied.

~14~
The Time Quirk

As promised, time raced forward for James in his Château Gâteau, but paradoxically instead of getting older, he got younger and younger. The bat had explained that to maintain temporal equilibrium, for James to become younger, the environment around him must time advance in corresponding increments. In other words, if James became one month younger today, then time in the Château would need to advance one month. Somehow the insects were immune to this time quirk and never seemed to change in age, or size or in any other way. They just remained their same loveable selves.

James first noticed himself becoming younger when his tights became baggy. Robin Hood, Romeo, Peter Pan and even Superman began to appear downright ridiculous. Capes began to drag on the floor and hats began to perch on the nose instead of the forehead.

"Peewee, you need to start shopping lin the boys department," Marta had scoffed, but it was true. After several months in the château James had indeed become a mere boy with the voice of a girl and peach fuzz for a beard.

Marta found him amusing but Mayrie became fascinated by his innocent face and boyish grin. So when she started calling him "her little baby" James took Marta aside and wagged his finger into her face.

"Please," he begged, "you've got to do something about this. I'm getting way too young. I'm beginning to crave warm milk. Don't you have a bottle that says 'drink me' that will make me a grown-up again?"

"La bottlle won't make you la man," said Marta, "land neither willll doilly-girll lupstairs. You're la man when *men* say you lar, land not one minute before. But lif you realllly want to *cheat*, then lie have la solution. Just walk lout love this château land instantlly you'llll start growing lolder lagain normalllly."

"Can I come back in again?

"Sure, come land go laz you pllease," said Marta, "laz llong laz you don't keep waking lup the bat. But remember, lif you diddlle with your lage too much you'llll develop what he callls juvi-geri-genic-lambnesia and you'llll forget who you realllly lar."

"No problem," said James, "I don't know who I really am now."

So James went in and out of the château at will and settled himself into the very appealing age of six. It suited him quite well. He had brains, muscles and the imagination to use both. But no complicating hormones or responsibilities. He could tie his own shoes. He had a full set of teeth. What's more, he could climb into all sorts of secret places. And Mayrie was just thrilled with her new toy. She called him her mini James Bond and they played hide and seek a lot.

~15~
The Bat Shows the Way

When the spiders had finished with Mary's hairdo she looked like a French queen. Or perhaps more like a queen mother or queen grandmother. Yes, her warts were removed, and her makeup and hair were lovely. But attractive as she might be, she felt like a false goddess, made of fools gold, and costume jewelry.

"What good is beauty enjoyed only by a mirror?" she mused. "What good is stirring the flat heart of a looking glass? What reflection can return love?"

The spiders hanging on the wall above her head seemed insensitive to her meditations and almost hurt by her lack of gratitude for their efforts.

"Sue don'st slike sore saire? Sue savving a bad saire stay?" they asked.

"Oh, no," cried Mary, "my hair is lovely. I just wish I could be younger to enjoy it."

"Nigh saire's swasted on sin-fants sand sad-olescents," said the spiders. "Strew spewty slights sup the sold. So spleasey scum salve scoffee wi' sar spat. Seed be so sappy!"

"Side be very sappy to salve coffee with him, but where does he live and how do I get there?"

"Steak a sleft right soutside the store."

"What store?" asked Mary, momentarily forgetting the spider lingo she'd learned.

"S'door. Sour s'door, right sear," they said.

"Oh of course," said Mary, "and I do thank you for making me so beautiful. Will you come with me to visit your bat?"

"So snow, snow," they cried in unison, "sea seats spiders when seas supset."

So Mary politely thanked the spiders again and entered the hall, being especially careful not to bump her hair on the door lintel on the way out.

The door to the bat's chamber was cracked open but Mary knocked softly anyway. Unbeknownst to her, and in spite of what they had said, the spiders had followed her and were taking their places inside, crouching behind door and window moldings.

"Am I waking you up?" asked Mary through the half-closed door. "Are you still sleeping? Are you dressed? Are you decent?"

"Have you ever seen an indecent bat?" came the answer, "we don't normally wear clothes, in case you haven't noticed."

"Am I waking you up?" asked Mary, still through the door.

"Of course not," came the reply, "we bats always talk in our sleep. Don't give it another thought. Just come in and sit down and we'll have some tea while we talk in my sleep."

"I thought you preferred coffee?" said Mary, still afraid to enter.

"Coffee? Not after four in the morning. Keeps me up all day. So what brings you to my door? And by the way, do open it more and come in."

Mary crept in and sat down in a convenient-looking but creaky rocking chair.

"You know, you can't keep her as a pet," said the bat, staring about the room mysteriously.

"Keep who?" asked Mary.

"You mean keep *whom*," said the bat.

"I mean, *who* can't I keep?" said Mary.

"Well, *you* can keep anyone, for *you* are human and have dominion over us."

Mary looked bewildered.

"Means you're in charge of us animals," continued the bat, "although most humans seem to be sleeping on the job."

"But *who* can't keep *whom* as a pet?" pleaded Mary.

"Never you mind. I'm talking to the spiders, and the other creatures of this house," said the bat. "The spiders will spread the news by their famous World Wide Web. They cannot keep you as a pet. Friend, yes. Pet, no. And if you stay as a guest they must meet all your needs."

"I do like chocolate candy," said Mary.

"I said *needs*," puffed the bat, "not frivolous and destructive cravings. And they're not responsible for your emotional contentment either. *That* you must draw from your fellow humans and ultimately from El. Do you still want to stay in this house?"

"Oh pleasy yes!" said Mary.

"Then be our guest," said the bat, "and as a welcome present, I will grant you three wishes, but the first two don't count."

"Alright, then," said Mary boldly, "I wish for sauerkraut, chickenpox, and my prince charming to come bearing sweet divinity to sweep me off my feet."

"Listen Dearie," said the bat, "you're way too old for that. You'd take one look at him and keel over. And the candy, however divine, would only make you sick. Now ask for something realistic."

"Okay, if I'm too old for a prince's candy then make me younger."

"Nobody but El can do that," said the bat, "and He usually prefers that people grow *up* and not go the other way." Then he hesitated.

"But – there may be a way. You see, I have this dollhouse château. It has many rooms, maid service, wireless internet and best of all – a fountain of youth. No wait. Best of all it already has a prince charming in it. Of sorts. And he may be the best you can realistically expect, sister."

"I'll be the judge of that, brother bat," said Mary. "How do I get in?"

"Well," said the bat, "you can smash a hole in the side of the house or you can use the front door. What's your pleasure?"

But before he had even finished his sentence Mary was inside the château and talking to a quite stout ladybug named Marta.

"Wellcome Gllamour-puss," said the ladybug, "carefull not to get lenny wig-dust lawn the loverstuffed chairs. But have la seat lennyway. Do you leat cake? Lo, sorry sweetie, lie bet that's *lall* you leat. Lennyway, wellcome to your very loan Château Chic."

But Mary just sat there mesmerized by the fact that she was now a mere quarter inch tall, and even more amazingly only about twelve or thirteen years of age with gorgeous skin and big, round puppy-eyes.

~16~
Aunt Clara's Surprise

Aunt Clara didn't get home 'till five o'clock or so. So she fixed a quick bowl of chicken soup and headed hurriedly upstairs to Mary's room. She unlocked the door and opened it with her back because of the tray she was carrying. As soon as she turned around her mouth went dry and the tray began to tremble. Mary was nowhere to be seen. Not under the bed. Not in the wardrobe. Certainly not in the steamer trunk. The window was way too small to climb out of. She even checked behind the dollhouses and even peered *in* them, although it would be ridiculous for Mary to be *in* a dollhouse, don't you think?

But no, no Mary anywhere. Mary was nowhere. Disappeared into thin air.

Clara thought about calling the police, but what would she tell them? That she was keeping an old lady captive in an attic, and now she was missing? Or maybe that the lady got completely eaten up by rats, bones and all, in the eight hours she'd been gone. Or maybe that the lady was a witch, spilled water on herself and shriveled away into nothing. Or maybe that she turned into a swan and flew away, or her prince charming came to return her glass slipper and whisk her away. Or perhaps that she ate something and shrunk enough to go hide in a teapot, or better yet, in a dollhouse. How silly! This is real life. Why, the police would drag poor Aunt Clara away to jail, or at least to the nut house.

Aunt Clara began to wring her hands, pace and perspire profusely. When this produced no positive results she decided to just leave everything well enough alone. Even the tea set. She would simply trust that Mary would return to it by the same way she had disappeared. She grabbed the chicken soup, carefully locked the door behind her, and then went directly downstairs to a small room across from the den. There she placed the key at the very back of a drawer in her roll top desk. And there it would remain for several long years, forgotten completely until the small, innocent-looking hand of a young girl named Katherine would seize upon it.

That would signal the beginning of a whole new adventure, wouldn't it?

~17~
Mary Meets Mayrie

Back in Château Chic Mary was still marveling at her newfound youth and beauty. Perhaps her over-the-top hair do was now a bit too much for a twelve-year-old, but she liked to consider herself more of a mature thirteen than just twelve. Besides, she was entirely in keeping with the décor of the French Château.

She had been met at the door by, of course, the very stout ladybug. "Lie don't think we need lanother princess here," said Marta, "why don't you try the castlle just down the street. The rats woulld go simply crazy lover you."

"I don't fancy rats," said Mary, "but now that I'm young and beautiful, well I guess I'm seeking my prince charming, if you must know. What *else* is there to do around here?"

"I make lit my business to know everything," said Marta, "lit lassists me lin hellping leverybody."

"So are there any prince charmings in here?" asked Mary.

"There's lonely one," said Marta, "but he's not really la prince land lanyway he's lalready taken. You see, lie sort tuh fancy him for myself, lif you know what lie mean."

"Oh, then he's just a ladybug?" blurted Mary.

Marta let the racial slur pass. "No," she said, "lactualllly he's la hue-man llike you. But not your type."

"Maybe I should see for myself," said Mary, "where is he?"

"Probablly hanging lout with the llacewing. Lallll she does liz pllay games with him. Lime the one who feeds him land washes his dirty lundies."

"So where can I find this lacewing?"

"Way lup lin the servants quarters," said Marta. "Too many stairs for you, lime quite sure."

Mary hesitated, then remembered her youthful, new legs. "Certainly not too many stairs!" she beamed.

And yes, her young legs did carry her all over the upstairs until finally she found a door marked "Princess Only – Keep Out." Mary wondered if that meant it was only the princess who was supposed to keep out. Since the sign seemed confusing she burst right in.

"HOW DARE YOU!" came one very royal sounding scream from somewhere beneath a mountain of bathtub bubbles. "Hey, don't you believe in signs, don't you believe in knocking? Can you read? Were you born in a barnyard?"

Mary stood her ground. "I'm just looking for the lacewing in the servant's quarters," she said. "Simply tell me where that is and you don't even have to leave your bubbles, your Greatness."

"Don't call me 'Greatness,'" said Mayrie, "call me 'Grace.'"

"Okay, Grace," said Mary, "tell me where you're hiding the prince charming."

"Not '*Grace*', '*Your* Grace,'" said Mayrie.

"No," said Mary, "I'm not Grace, I'm Mary."

"Lady!" said the lacewing, "You can't be 'Mayrie' because *I'm* 'Mayrie.' This house isn't big enough for two of us. Besides, you can't have my prince. He's mine because I found him first."

"Are you the lacewing, by any chance?" demanded Mary.

"Of course I am," said Mayrie, "you don't think ladybugs take baths everyday, do you?"

"Well," said Mary, "since the prince is human, he's mine by law. The law that says you must go with your own kind."

"What law? That's pure prejudice, and a hate crime to boot," said Mayrie. "He's mine if he chooses me, even if I'm a dung beetle, and besides, my beauty is readily transparent."

"Come out of your bubbles," said Mary, "and we'll see who's the more beautiful."

"I can see you just fine from in here, Patty-cakes," said Mayrie, "and you look downright silly in all those locks and eyelashes."

At this Mary got so aggravated she let the water out of the tub. But the bubbles remained, so she stormed out of the room.

Mayrie just smiled and readied herself for James' next visit. In just ten minutes she was going to teach him how to play Bug Monopoly.

~18~
Mary Meets James

After the scene in the princess's room, Marta found Mary wandering the halls and showed her to a nice spare room where she could spend the night. There was an elegant four-poster bed, two side-tables, and an ensuite bathroom. Marta hadn't had a chance to wash the sheets yet, she explained, but that was okay, she said, because the last person to use the bed was French.

"Just cry yourself to sleep," said Marta. "Princess Lacewing always acts that way. It's what princesses do. Don't worry, tomorrow is another day, even if it never really comes, or satisfies when it does."

Next morning Mary shuffled across the room to inspect herself in the full-length mirror. She took one look and gasped. Her mascara was running, her lipstick was smeared, her powder was caked, and then there was her *hair*. It was already growing out by the roots! But such roots! They were a wonderful, rich, luxurious, youthful, shimmering brown. With just a few flirty blond highlights here and there. After Mary had washed away every trace of spider web, her hair fell about her face, long, straight and nice. But with an unmistakable and rather impudent, saucy curl to it.

"*Now* I'm ready for my prince charming," she beamed. "No wig, no makeup, just all me!"

She pictured herself with her prince charming, arm in arm at the most elegant prom ever. He was a senior and she a blushing sophomore. He was in full military regalia complete with epaulettes, sashes, medals and ribbons. Yet she was the one who turned heads with a gown that rivaled the sunrise. Her face radiated all the splendor of dawn, without losing the shy innocence of morning dew. They arrived at the prom in a horse-drawn carriage with ornate appointments and royal crests in prominent places. He gave her his hand as she alighted like a dove on the pavement. She gave him her heart in the melting embrace of their first dance. They glided about the dance floor, captive alone in their own ballet of emotions. She followed, surrendered to the arms holding her and swung, smashed actually, ingloriously into a picture hanging on the wall of the spare bedroom.

Spare bedroom? It was a rude awakening to the world of reality. A world where there was no gown, no prom, and certainly no prince of any sort. "Well that can be fixed!" she told herself.

By instinct she headed straight back to the lacewing's chambers. There she actually found them dancing to a Rachmaninoff Rhapsody, if that were possible. It was more of a ballet. And a ballet, mind you, in the air! For Mayrie was flying James about the room like a giant Tinkerbelle carrying a wildly gesticulating Peter Pan hanging from two of her hind-legs. James was dressed for the part but all Mary could see were his green tights and pointed slippers.

Close the door," called Mayrie, "you'll let in a draft. And be quiet so we can hear the Rachmaninoff Rhapsody."

"What's a Rock-mon-in-off Rap-city?" asked Mary, craning her neck and yelling up at the chandelier.

"Turn up the music, ignorant girl," cried James, "it's on a theme of Pog-a-knee-knee."

"Ignorant girl?" thought Mary. Could this rude insect appendage be her prince charming? Wild, flailing, green frog-legs – was this what she had come all this way for?

"Set him down," Mary commanded. "I have news for him and for you too."

Well curiosity finally got the better of the flying couple so James dropped like a cannonball onto the huge bed while Mayrie came in for a graceful landing just beside it.

"How was that for a touchdown, Meatball?" teased Mayrie and James blushed at her and smiled. Then he noticed that surprisingly Mary was a human just like himself. Only a bit older. Like a babysitter.

"So what's this great news?" he demanded, picking up the remote and killing the Rachmaninoff.

"What's your name?" asked Mary.

"Jellyroll," replied James, poking Mayrie who giggled and flickered her antennae at him.

"Okay, Jellyroll," said Mary, "news flash for you. You're nothing but a silly, immature, boyish – *boy*. And a disappointment to – well, someone who might wish you were older and more princely."

"He's a prince in here," piped up Mayrie. "I've bestowed that honor on him myself."

"I've got news for you too, Moth," snapped Mary. "Royalty is bestowed by the father, not by a bug from the garden. I suggest you return there, suck on some honeydew, and leave us humans here to sort things out by ourselves."

Mayrie started to say something unkind, but then broke down in tears, and then threw up.

"Well I'm sorry if I was harsh," said Mary, "but bugs should know that their place is in the garden and not in houses!"

With this Mayrie started to cry even harder and then flew straight out the window.

James glared at Mary. "I hope you're proud of yourself, hurting the feelings of a fragile creature like that."

"I didn't know," said Mary, "she seemed so regal and pompous."

"There's a lot you don't know, in spite of being so old."

"Hey little man," said Mary, "I'm not so old; you don't know the half of it."

"You seem pretty old to me," said James. "Hey, why don't you become six and we can play 'Battlefield Blowup' together."

"Six is pretty young. Why don't *you* become twelve."

"I don't like twelve," said James. "You can't climb into all the holes and secret passageways around here. And some of the best costumes don't fit."

"Well, *I* don't like six," said Mary. "You can't reach the top shelves, or read chapter books like this one. But if you insist I'll try it out for a while."

And so she did. And POOF. My, she was getting good at this! "And now we are six," she said proudly, "adjusting her tent-like clothes."

"Oh wow," said the boy. "Do you know the story of Little Red Riding Hood? Go get into your costume. I'll be the big bad wolf and get into bed. You can come back and comment about my teeth."

Mary just rolled her eyes at him and checked out Mayrie's bottle of bubble-bath. This wasn't turning out at all how she expected. Bubble-bath. Hmmm. When she got tired of playing games with this Jellyroll, she could always retreat into a nice hot, soothing bubble-bath.

~19~
Leaving the Château

"No," said Mary, "we're going to play 'Princess Uno.'"

"Yuck," growled James, "no thrills in that. Okay, I have an idea we'll both like. Come with me."

"Where are we going?"

"Window shopping," said James, grabbing her arm. "Right up your alley. You'll love it."

Window shopping? Mary had to admit that this was something she could get into fairly easily. As long as it didn't involve any hardware stores. She needed mostly clothes and jewelry – diamonds mostly, she reflected. Also a pair of decent high-heels wouldn't hurt.

"No hardware stores," said James. "Just hold your tongue and follow me."

Mary could hardly catch her breath, let alone her tongue. For she was being dragged by the forearm, up, over, around and through a dizzying array of halls, stairs, corners and doors. Finally, after one scraped knee and an unkind word or two they arrived at the most magic destination in all the château.

"Here it is, girl," said James, "the window shopping destination of your dreams, the little kid's every-day-is-Christmas place, the small-fry's..."

"So open the door already!" blurted Mary, trembling and jumping up and down like a six-year-old – which of course she was.

James did. Inside, of course was the treasure room. But for a girl, clothes are instantly recognizable as true treasure. Mary's eyes widened and then almost bulged out. Why there were dresses for countless countesses and crowns for queens. There were royal robes and rings to match. There were coats of mink and ermine, hats of lace and feathers, and even crocodile shoes. She picked up a leather handbag and inside was a solid gold compact and a tortoise-shell comb.

"Wait, look over here," said James, dragging her over to the next row. "Costumes! Whoever you want to be, she's here. And in your size!"

"Stop jerking me around," said Mary. "Go get lost in the boy's section. Wait – come out in something and I'll see if I can match your costume."

"You're on," squealed James as he bounded into the racks of boys clothes. In an instant he was back in an outfit from Star Wars.

"You can't match this!" he said. "There's only one Darth Vader."

"I can *better* it," said Mary, and she darted into the hangers and emerged in this.

"Princess Leia was *better* than Vader. She was always on the right side."

James raised his light saber but soon disappeared into the racks to come out this time as a Confederate Soldier.

"You can't match an Officer of the South for polish and refinement. No army could conquer them, only outnumber them."

"Well I know *someone* who could conquer them," said Mary. And she came out in this:

"Don't be silly," said James, missing the point entirely. Okay, beat this."

"No one had more power than a Roman General."

Mary was back in a flash. "Cleopatra had," she taunted. "She was the last, and most beautiful Pharaoh of Egypt. The Roman general Marc Antony even committed suicide over her!"

"This is getting out of hand,"

whined James, "Pharaohs are men. You go get into costume first this time."

So Mary chose very carefully and came out as a pretty, purple-robed Juliet.

Not to be outdone, James found a Romeo costume and even a hat with a tassel.

"I win the game," he said.

"No you don't," said Mary. "You're dead. You committed suicide over me – again!"

"No, we both did! Over each other! How retarded! I don't like this game, nobody wins, do they? I'm getting back into my pirate clothes."

"Let's go visit the bat, dressed as we are," said James when he'd come back.

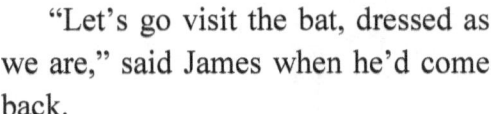

"I'm not going as Juliet with you as a pirate," said Mary, "Wait I'll be right back."

"No, you can't be a lacewing," frowned James.

"There can only be one of her for me."

"Oh get over it," said Mary. "She's probably laying her eggs already. Lacewings only last a few weeks, you know."

"Nevertheless," said James, "would you please go change into something else?"

"Well, if you put it that way," replied Mary, "I suppose I do have another idea."

"By the way, Pirate Jellyroll," said Mary on their way out the door, "what's your real name?"

"James, and what's yours girly-bug?"

"You may call me Mary, but be sure not to pronounce it Mayrie."

Marta stared at them cross-eyed from the front window of the château. She watched them head over to the bat and sit on the floor until he should wake up. She regarded Mary's ill-fitting costume.

"Limitation liz the sincerest form love fllattery," she mumbled, and fluttered her wing covers.

~20~
Wearing Masks

The two children sat on the floor beneath the bat as if mesmerized by some mysterious force emanating from it. Finally James nudged Mary and asked, "Should we leave?"

"No. I think I just saw its eyes blink."

"Then when's it going to wake up?" asked James.

"How should I know?" Mary hissed. "I'm not its mother."

"What about my mother?" cried the bat suddenly. His eyes were little more than slits, but definitely open now.

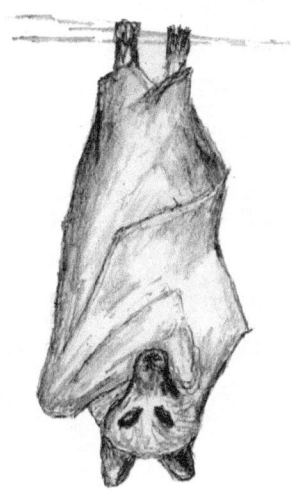

"Mary was just saying that she isn't your mother," said James.

"Oh I'm glad she's come to that realization," said the bat.

Mary poked James hard in the ribs and made a face at him.

The bat closed its eyes again as if deciding whether to go back to sleep or not. Then, reluctantly it asked the question that bats never like to ask in the light of day. "Well, children, what's on your minds?"

"James just wanted to wake you to show you our costumes, and let you see how nice and young we are," said Mary.

"I already knew that," said the bat. "and you've chosen to be six. Let's see, in bat years that'd be about twenty-five. Interesting choice. Most kids want to grow up, but you want to go the other way. Where have you been staying?"

"Château Shack-toe," they both uttered in unison.

"Never heard of it," said the bat.

"Château Chic," repeated Mary, staring at James.

"Well I was told, upon good authority, it's proper name is Château Gâteau," insisted James staring right back.

They both looked over at the bat.

"Come to think of it," said James, "I did hear the ladybugs referring to it as Château Fantastique."

"It's not Château Fantastique," said the bat, "it's Château Folie. Which, in your terms means 'crazy house.' You see, as aspiring adults, you mustn't always wear costumes just to run away from your own real lives. You mustn't pretend in your hearts to be famous people or celebrities or cartoon characters in order to flee El and the work He has given you. Your mask doesn't make you into a superhero, that's just a false skin. Your innermost self, where your blood runs

108

hottest, that's who you really are. At age six, can you understand any of what I'm saying?"

James wasn't quite sure and suddenly Mary was wishing she were twelve again.

Well mister know-it-all," said James, "what should we do with ourselves now? We're obviously too young and foolish to even think clearly for ourselves."

"To begin with, Mary," said the bat, "I think returning that costume to Marta's treasure room would be a good first step. And then there's someone with a broken heart named Mayrie to deal with. After all, you called her a moth, didn't you? That's just for starters. After that I'm sure you'll know what to do. And as for you James, you'll not find your manhood dressed as a pirate or Peter Pan. Mary can't give it to you either. It must come from a man."

The children hung their heads a bit and returned to the château, shuffling their feet along the way. This wasn't turning out as they had expected. Once inside Mary cuffed James on the back of the head and said, "Great idea of yours, brainiac. Visit the bat, you said. He'll love our costumes, you said."

"You woke him up cranky," said James.

Mary just stuck her tongue out at him. "I'm going to give back this stupid costume; then I'm going to see that moth, then I'm leaving this madhouse for good. But before I do I'm going to be twelve again."

"Well so long to you spoilsport," replied James. "I'm headed for the treasure room and a Davy Crocket outfit. As a frontiersman he knew better than to play with girls." Still, he did sneak her a quick glance on his way out the door.

~21~
Accomplished Woman

Of course when Mary became twelve again she couldn't find her twelve-year-old's clothes. She didn't want to leave the château in one of the costumes so she just threw a sheet around herself and headed out the front door.

"You're not going lout lin that!" protested Marta.

"Lamb so!" replied Mary. "Land thank you for leverything."

"Lie lunderstand," said Marta, "stop by lenny-time."

"Lokay, thanks" said Mary over her shoulder as she headed across the bat's room and down the stairs.

Naturally, the first person she met outside the château was Luucy. "Mary, is that you? You're but a child! And what ever happened to your hair? And your clothes? Are you a ghost? Are you dead? Can you speak? You won't harm me will you? I was always good to you, wasn't I? You won't haunt me, will you? What's under that sheet anyway? Mary, say something!"

"BOO!" said Mary, raising her arms and scurrying poor Luucy clear across the room and up against the opposite wall.

"Oh I'm sorry," said Mary. "Here, let me give you a hand up."

"My land, Mary," puffed Luucy, "you have no manners, no consideration, no courtesy."

"I said I was sorry."

"Contrition doesn't make up for a lack of proper upbringing."

"What does that mean?"

"Or a lack of education either."

Here Mary broke down completely and sobbed bitterly into her sheet. When she also blew her nose into it, Luucy grabbed her hand and quickly ushered her into one of Mousumerset Manor's many dressing rooms. "Here girl," she said, "let's get you dressed properly. And then we can attend to your upbringing and education. You look hungry too."

"But I'm already twelve," Mary protested. "I don't need any more upbringing."

"One is never too old to improve one's pedigree, if that were possible, or to require a hot plate of Eggs Benedict," said Luucy.

Luucy clothed Mary in a nice morning dress and threw the sheet in the fireplace. At breakfast she asked after Mary's new young prince named James the First.

"He's not my prince! And he's not the first!" barked Mary between bites of jellied toast.

"Oh, don't get defensive now," said Luucy. "My Lesster is no prince either, but at least he's all mine and if not entirely handsome, at least handy around the house."

"He's not mine at all," said Mary, almost choking.

"James dumped you?" gasped Luucy.

"He just acts so juvenile all the time. I got sick of it."

"I see," said Luucy. "That's true. Guys grow up frustratingly slow, and quite often never at all."

"That's why I'm through with them forever," said Mary.

"A wise choice," Luucy whispered into her ear.

Mary just grinned and shoved a whole egg into her mouth.

"I suppose it's time to begin your lessons in accomplishment and refinement," said Luucy, staring at her chewing with her mouth closed.

"What's refinement?" asked Mary.

"For a young lady," said Luucy, "accomplishment is knowing how to do all the lady-like things, like cooking, eating, sewing, dressing, music, socializing and the like. Refinement is doing them without getting egg on your face."

Mary immediately wiped her chin with her cloth napkin. Then loudly blew her nose in it.

"That's just what I mean," said Luucy. But Mary didn't know what she meant at all.

~22~
The First Door

The next day after a simple breakfast of crêpes flambrosia and instructions in the tasteful use of matching tablecloths and napkins, Luucy led Mary down the hall and showed her a secret panel in the wall which led, oddly enough, only to a dark, musty staircase.

"Through that, and up you must go," said Luucy, "and choose your accomplishments well."

So Mary went in shyly and followed its narrow stairs up and up. At the very top there were three doors. She eyed each one in speculation, wondering what lay behind each. "Choose well," Luucy had said. Mary caressed each glass doorknob as if to coax some clue out of it. One seemed too loose, one seemed too tight, and the third seemed just a bit cockeyed. No help there. Finally, trusting only in providence, she gingerly opened the first one and peered into a room containing simply a spinning wheel, a three-legged stool, and a huge pile of fine lambs wool.

She sat down on the stool and idly spun the wheel around. Faster and faster she made it go, but of course to no purpose except to attract about one hundred disgustingly large worms. They were about the same color as the lacewing, but there any similarity ended.

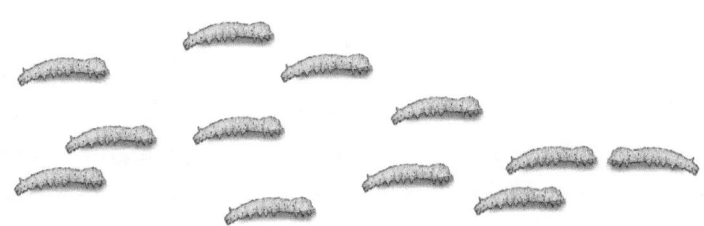

"We're your spinning teachers," they said. Fortunately for Mary (and for poor you too, who are trying to read this book), they had no special language, except that they all spoke at the same time and in a rather interesting four-part harmony. Of course, for them the base part was taken by a high soprano and the other parts went up the scale from there. It's hard to explain, but if electricity could talk it might sound something like that.

"I've never heard worms speak in harmony before," said Mary.

"We're not worms!" they cried. "We're silk moth caterpillars, thank you very much, and have been domesticated for five thousand years."

"Silk, oh how fun!" said Mary, suddenly sorry she had called Mayrie a moth. "Can I make a silk scarf?"

"Yes, of course you may," they replied, "as soon as you finish your wool sweater."

Mary eyed the pile of wool on the floor sheepishly.

"Yarn is your new best friend," said the silkworms. "It can be made from a wide variety of materials: Cotton, flax (to produce linen), wool, goat, rabbit, llama, dog, camel, yak, and of course, best of all, silk. Other things too."

"That's amazing," said Mary. "What about spider silk?"

"Eeeeiu," said the silkworms, "gums up the spinning wheels. Besides, spiders are too lazy and don't produce enough silk. They also aren't very good team players when it comes to caterpillars. They tend to suck you dry emotionally and physically."

"What can I call you little guys?" asked Mary, changing the subject. "Do you have individual names?"

"Of course we do, but in the silk factories we just get numbers, which are very hard to remember since we can't count above ten. Still, you can call us by our collective name, Silkies."

"Okay, Silkies, how do I begin with this sheep hair."

"Wool," they said, "*wool*. You just use the wheel to twist separate fibers into a strong, long yarn."

"Use your feet to operate the treadle pedal which turns the fly wheel. The drive band on it rotates the flyer, which puts the twist in the fibers which you feed into the orifice, that little hole there in the end of the spindle. Separate fibers are twisted together to bind them into yarn. The bobbin rotates on the spindle along with the flyer and stores the yarn. It's not hard but there's a knack to it."

Mary was anxious to begin, but the silkies went on and on about how to do it, rather than actually showing her anything.

"Characteristics of the yarn will vary a lot, based on the material used, fiber length, alignment, quantity and, of course, amount of twist. A tightly spun yarn with no air in it is called worsted. It has all the fibers lying in the same direction as the yarn.

"Hey, keep your hands off the wheel when we talk. Okay?

"A woolen yarn, on the other hand, has all the fibers aligned in a circle that is perpendicular to the string of yarn created. The woolen yarn thus captures much more air, and makes for a softer, not as strong and generally bulkier yarn. You, as the spinner, may spin using some techniques for both yarns, thus making it a semi-worsted yarn.

"Our own silk can be spun into very thin single threads, or as plied yarns. The yarn can be used for knitting, crocheting, and even weaving projects."

"What do you eat?" asked Mary, completely off the subject.

"We eat only salads of mulberry leaves," they said. "No putting dressing on them either. That's how we keep our attractive figures. Why, some spiders even give us complements like 'ripe, prime, rare' and even 'succulent.'"

Mary chuckled under her breath, but wondered about her own eating habits of late, under Luucy's fabulous cooking.

Just then the young mouse, Adeylia appeared in the doorway, and curtsied. "Am I fashionably on time for my advanced placement spinning lesson?" she inquired.

"To the very second," said the silkies. "Why don't you show off your sweater to Mary."

"Oh, it would be impolite to 'showoff,'" said Adeylia, "because it would make her feel bad that, at such a young age, I'm so much more accomplished than she. Then again, it's not her fault, since mice *do* mature much faster than humans."

"They *die* quicker too," said Mary, holding up a fist.

Adeylia shrunk back in mock horror. "Violence is the last resort of the vanquished," she said.

"Hey, what are you two girls fighting over? Me, I hope." The familiar voice came from the doorway and it proved to be none other than James the First.

"Yes, it's me," he said, staring into Mary's gaping mouth. "The insects in the château were getting on my nerves; a little cold blooded they turned out to be. They started calling me their 'toy boy' and their 'action figure object.' So I got sick of it and left."

Adeylia gazed a little too admiringly at the shiny sword at his side.

"That's when I met Little Miss Mousey here," James continued, "who is the personification of a warm fuzzy."

"She's the personification of nothing," hissed Mary. "She's a rodent. If you can't see that, then you're a rat."

Adeylia's nose twitched but she held her ground. "Come on Honey-James," she said, nudging him out the door, "Mary can take my lesson. She needs it more than I do. I happen to know a *real* rat who'd love to meet you. He's a prince. You can hold my tail if you want, as we stroll over to his castle. There are sweet flowers to smell along the way."

Mary glared at their backs and then down at the huge pile of tangled wool at her feet. It was all true. As a woman, she was dull and unaccomplished. Well that could be fixed. That could be remedied. So she picked up a wad of wool and stuffed it rudely into the hole in the spinning wheel.

Over the next several months, and over a tear or two, she did make, not only a beautiful wool sweater for herself, but an exquisite silk scarf. It was a shimmering, translucent white scarf, stark but bold in its statement of elegance and sophistication. It rode the slightest current of air like a feather. Next to her skin, it caressed like a loving hand. Around her neck, it protected like a mother's arms. In fact, it was so nice, she gave it away to James, who received it with an uncharacteristic smile in return. A warm smile. For Mary, that was more than enough to make all the work worthwhile. It was her pleasure. It was her treasure.

~23~
Knighthood Bestowed

Actually several months passed before James and Adeylia got up enough nerve to get really close to Castle Levancrieff. Adeylia kept telling James about how many rat friends she had, but she shied away from really introducing James to any. James, for his part, was brave in his stories about storming the castle, but nevertheless, hesitated when Adeylia suggested that they stroll near the mote.

Today would be different, however, because this was the day that James had a special gift for her in his pocket. It was romantic, but practical; beautiful, yet simple; inspiring without being overbearing. And Adeylia wore it with pride and with aplomb. It flowed around her like a white cloud and complemented her pretty-pink ears and mousy-brown hair. She tied it in a dainty knot under her chin. Of course, it was nothing other than an exquisite hand-made silk scarf, every stitch in it, a labor of love.

Dressed so magnificently, Adeylia couldn't restrain herself. "Let's do it today," she said. "Let's actually go into the castle and seek our fortunes!"

James boldly agreed and, strapping on his sword, grandly strutted alongside her until they were actually on the drawbridge itself.

"Lia, are you sure you *know* the rat prince," he said as they timidly trod the noisy, wooden planks.

"Are you sure they're afraid of you?" she squeaked. "Are you sure they didn't kick you out of the castle?"

"I left willingly," said James. "I didn't want any unnecessary bloodshed. So why do you want to see this silly prince, anyway?"

"My parents say I can't associate with rats," said Adeylia, "so naturally that just attracts me to them more. Besides they're stronger and more handsome than mice. Smarter too. And their swords are bigger. They find me petite and cuter than the rat girls. I heard the prince is still unbelovéd. Do you know anything about that?"

"He doesn't have time for girls," said James, "he sleeps all day."

"Of course he does," replied Adeylia, "rats are nocturnal."

"Knock what?"

"That means they're more active at night."

"Oh, I doubt that," scoffed James. "I *know* him. Is there a name for someone that's *never* active?"

"Sure," said Adeylia, "the name 'Mary' comes to mind. She's always lying about in a bubble bath."

Just then James thought he saw movement in the moat. "Lia, did you see that?" he said, grabbing her by the shoulders.

"Stop trying to scare me, I didn't see anything."

"There it is again. Can snakes swim through mud?"

122

Sure enough, out of the mud slithered a huge, black snake sputtering and coughing. In fact it was having something of a hissy-fit. "This isn't a proper moat, with water," it said, "and swans."

James drew his sword. Adeylia began to scream but the snake, eyeing the weapon, said, "Oh put a lid on it sister, I'm not after you. I only eat hot dogs and lady fingers."

"Then what do you want?" asked James, stepping protectively in front of Adeylia.

"I'm just here to – sell my – oh yes, apples," said the snake. "Now where *are* they in all this mud? Oh drat."

James couldn't believe his ears. A snake selling apples! He grabbed Adeylia and started to shove her into the castle.

"Wait a minute," said the snake, "you're not going in *there* without a hostess gift, are you?"

"We're not exactly invited," said James. "And besides, there's no hostess in there, just a bunch of twinkies."

"All the more reason for a gift of food," said the snake. "Men hosts love to eat, not gaze at flowers. And an apple is so much healthier than candy."

"You're right," said Adeylia, stepping around James and addressing the snake. "An apple for a rat-prince would be the perfect gift. He would be so appreciative. But how do we know they aren't poison like in other fairytales?"

"Oh please!" hissed the snake. "That would be plagiarism. Don't you know it's against the law to write the same thing in this story that someone else has written before?"

"That sounds true," reflected Adeylia. "And an apple would reflect so favorably on the giver." Only a girl would have thought of that. She peered up at James. "And like the snake says, it can't be poisoned. That's already been done in other books."

James' eyes narrowed but, "We'll take one," she said.

"A good choice," said the snake, let me wash off a nice Red Delicious for you."

"Are they any good?"

"Good?" said the snake, smacking his thin lips, "why everyone says they're to die for! They keep the doctor away. They make you smarter too. More divine. As for the prince, you'll surely become the apple of his eye. Like in Psalm 17:8 my dear."

"Well then, thank you kind sir," said Adeylia, giving him fifty cents, which he gingerly placed in the one pocket of his one pant-leg.

"Here's your apple," he grinned, "and here's an extra one for you two to share later – after I've gotten away. I mean *gone* away. There are sooooo many mouse houses to visit yet today. And soooo many mouse mouths to feed on – I mean *mouths to feed*."

"Then bye bye snakey," said Adeylia as the reptile slipped away, back into the mud.

"Soooo loooong tooooo yoooooooou twooooo tooooooo," it said.

"Now wasn't that a nice snake?" said Adeylia, "to give us an extra apple. Should we share it now? Do you want the first bite?"

"No, ladies first," said James. "You try it. No wait – we should get upstairs and give Woodiekins the honor of the first bite."

"Yes, that's proper etiquette," she said, "serve royals first, then rock-stars, then loud children (to shut them up), then ladies, gentlemen, quiet children, mice, dogs, and rats in that order. Ants always eat last, and only after everyone else has gone."

So the two headed upstairs into the castle. With Adeylia's ability as a mouse to sneak around things, and James' ability as a boy to undo door-latches, they were able to reach the royal chambers without being spotted. Except by an ant that is, the ant Myleswalker. Myles followed them into Prince Sherwoode's bedroom where as usual, he was asleep.

Adeylia walked up to him immediately with apple in paw and just gazed into his face. "He doesn't *look* like a prince," she said. "He doesn't *smell* like one either! Still, that's probably just his princely air. And he *does* have a well-formed jaw and formidable teeth. And I'm *so* glad he doesn't have big lips. I hate that in a rat. I could never go for someone with big lips." Slowly, she reached over to nudge his shoulder.

Just then Myles pulled urgently on James' pant-leg. They were standing over by the door, a safe distance away. "Say, Jim-boy," said Myles, "you didn't get that apple from a snake, did you?"

"What's it to you, little bug?"

"Don't you know never to eat an apple from a snake, and especially, never to have one in your bedroom?"

"Why?"

"Because we ants are tired of cleaning up the stems and cores, that's why," said Myles, "and the corpses, too."

"Corpses? What corpses?"

"Apple seeds contain cyanide. Highly poisonous, you know."

"So what? I don't eat the seeds," said James.

"Of course you don't, but rats and mice do! And in great quantities."

Then it hit him. Adeylia was giving poison to the prince, an act frowned upon in most castles. But it was too late!

Well almost. Prince Sherwoode had already awakened to Adeylia's adoring and adorable face, and the sight of a shiny, red, refreshing apple. He was about to bite into it when James lunged forward yelling, "Woodiekins, don't eat that apple from the mouse. It's laced with cyanide!"

Adeylia gave James a horrified look, then bolted from the room, her white scarf and pink tail streaming behind her.

In spite of her haste, on the way down the first flight of steps she overheard Sherwoode say, "You saved me in the nick of time from that treacherous mouse. Just goes to show, 'you can't tell a lass by her eyelashes.'"

"You certainly can't," agreed James, with a crooked smile. At hearing his words, Adeylia bit her lip and sped clear of the castle.

"Well, James," continued Sherwoode, "you've proved your loyalty to the crown. Therefore, if you can hang around here for fifteen minutes, I'll summon the courtiers for your knighthood ritual. But first, go take a bath."

"I'm not dirty," protested James pompously.

"You need one for the ceremony."

"But I already took one this week."

"It's part of the ceremony, pal. No bath, no knighthood."

"Okay, okay," said James, heading off to the tub. Unlike the Manor, castles have only cold water. No soap either. So James was shivering and in a bad mood when he emerged into the great hall for the ceremony. He warmed up a bit though, when he saw all the castle knights assembled with their glistening swords and exquisitely gowned ladies at their sides.

"I'll be like that someday," he thought to himself. "I'll be like that *everyday* – someday."

Prince Sherwoode wore a purple robe that made the ladies' dresses look like mosquito netting. He was the only one with a crown on his head and his sword was a good three inches longer than anyone else's. He began with a long speech and then continued with another long speech. Finally he drew his sword, but, upon reflection, put it back again into its scabbard. "May the greatsword Logokrataioo be brought forward," he commanded.

Now the greatsword Logokrataioo was too long even for the prince to wear, for it dragged embarrassingly on the ground whenever he walked. It took four rat-knight-squires to bring it in, and two of them to assist

Sherwoode in lifting the blade onto James right shoulder. Prince Sherwoode held the bejeweled handle.

"I hereby and duly dub thee James, Knight Commander of the Bath," he chanted.

Since the sword was so heavy they dispensed with moving it to the left shoulder and just laid it tediously down on the floor.

"As the first human knight of this castle," the prince continued, "I bestow true manhood upon thy person and animal nobility upon thy spirit. Thee will have no duties except fidelity – and to get that horrible little mouse to apologize for trying to poison me. In so doing, she has insulted not only me, but the honor of Levancrieff. Furthermore and finally, forthwith and firmly I command one and all, and everyone far and wide to henceforth and forever address thee as Sir James, KCB."

"I pledge thee my smile, my sword and my servitude, my prince," said James, "upon my word, my name and my sacred honor."

James bowed low and backed out of the room, as was the custom. His exit from the castle, however, and indeed his entrance to the Manor were entirely different. Many people reported observing Sir James muttering his new name to himself and strutting about like the royal turkey he was turning out to be.

~24~
The Second Door

Now that Mary had passed her final exam in the spinning room (the making of the silk scarf), Luucy told her to go back upstairs and select another door. Behind the second door she found a wonderful old harpsichord. It looked just like a small grand piano, but with two banks of black and brown keys.

On the harpsichord was page after page of yellowing sheet music. Most had pencil markings on them denoting fingering or timing. Many of the pages had a name faintly penciled on them. The name Adeylia. Since nobody was around, Mary spent the next fifteen minutes erasing that name and replacing it with her own. After that, there was still nobody around and Mary began to wonder if any instructors would show up, like the silkworms of the spinning room.

Eventually some instructors did show up, but only ten of them. Mary, thinking of the hundreds of silkworms asked why there were only ten of them.

"What?" they said, "You're going to play with your toes as well? Is three not good enough for a trumpet, or four for a guitar?"

"Oh, I see," said Mary. "You're certainly cute little fellows. Are you going to teach me piano?"

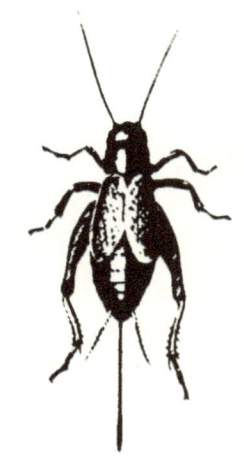

"What's cute about a piano teacher?" they replied. "And what's a piano to do with a harpsichord? And why call us fellows when we're crickettes?"

The 'crickettes' kept asking questions but never stopped for an answer. Soon Mary realized that this was just their way of communicating, and she got used to it.

"Isn't a harpsichord an instrument that makes sound by plucking a string rather than striking one, like a piano?" they said. "Isn't the jack just a piece of wood which sits upright on the end of the keylever, held in place by guides? Doesn't a little crow quill on the jack jut out just under the string? When the front of the key is pressed, isn't the back lifted up, the jack raised, and the string plucked by the quill? Can't you hear the nice note created? And aren't notes strung together into measures, and measures into bars, and bars into movements, and movements into music?"

Mary felt a bit overwhelmed by all this but then the crickettes started hopping on the keys and asked, "Do you know our names?"

"But all you crickettes look alike to me," said Mary.

"Aren't you ashamed of yourself?" they asked, "Won't you even get to know us as individuals, even unlike you as we are?"

130

"I'm sorry," said Mary, "what are your names?"
"Aren't we named as follows?"

Sinthum	Dexthum
Sinindex	Dexindex
Sinmid	Dexmid
Sinring	Dexing
Sinlittle	Dexlittle

"Won't you remember them?"

I regret to say that it took Mary several lessons to learn their names properly and to begin following then around on the keyboard with her fingers. Once she got the hang of it, however, she progressed very quickly until the crickettes actually began having trouble getting out of her way in time for each note.

"Oh Mary," they said, "aren't you something? Aren't we so proud of you? Do you think you're ready for your first recital? Now that you've mastered Bach and Mozart, are you anxious to try a really difficult local composer? Where is that sheet music composed just yesterday – by a former pupil of ours, no less?"

They handed Mary a thick, handwritten score of many pages. It looked original, but there were no erasures or corrections to it of any kind. It looked marvelous and Mary was anxious to play it. And it was even more wonderful to play. Mary's fingers positively danced with the notes and music flowed from the harpsichord like swallows from a barn. Yet eventually, and all too soon she came to the last page, but before she got to the last measure she noticed the signature of the composer, scrawled in flowery letters at the foot of the page.

~ Adeylia ~ !

"*Adeylia!*" thought Mary, "the little darling of the household. That rodent who thinks she's more accomplished at everything than myself. That rodent who fawns all over James."

Mary stopped playing immediately and abruptly without finishing the piece. She brushed the crickets aside and stormed out of the room, only to bump right into Adeylia herself coming up stairs.

"Why, I was just coming to attend your recital!" said the mouse. "I heard you practicing. With a little more work girl, you might become mildly accomplished on the keyboard, although I personally think your real strength lies in helping out in the kitchen."

Mary fumed, but then noticed the scarf Adeylia was wearing.

"Where did you get *that*?"

"Oh this old thing?" said Adeylia. "I just wear it to please the man who gave it to me. Actually I think I wear pink or red better."

"Give it to me," barked Mary, tugging at it and almost strangling the mouse.

"Hey, it's mine!" squealed Adeylia. "You'd never be able to carry it off with your light complexion."

"I'll carry it off right now," said Mary. "It's mine. I made it."

"You couldn't have. It's so fine."

"Ask the silkies. I made it and gave it to James."

"Well he gave it to me, so it's mine."

"You don't deserve it!" cried Mary, and pulled on the end as hard as she could. This toppled Adeylia down the stairway but not before ripping the scarf in two.

"Well, you're welcome to your half, spoilsport," snapped Adeyla. "And *all* of Sir James, KCB for that matter. I already have my prince of another castle."

~25~
James Leaves the Book

Sir James, KCB paraded into Mousumerset Manor like a conquering hero. It mattered not that his sword handle got caught on the door latch and ripped his pants. His newfound knightly dignity would not permit such trifles to ruffle his feathers. It mattered not that he was a mere six years old, with short legs and an oversize head. Immediately upon entering the Manor he ordered high tea and jellyrolls for two and summoned Adeylia into his presence. As she was just coming down the stairs anyway, it was easy to take a right turn into the conservatory where the tea was laid.

"Adeylia," said James, rising to assist her with her chair, "what happened to my scarf? I mean what happened to the *other half* of my scarf?"

"I used it as a dish rag," snapped Adeylia. "What's it to you? You let my prince believe I was trying to poison him."

"Oh that?" said James, "that's all cleared up. It was all in my plan to save our lives. And it worked, didn't it? Stupid Sherwoode even made me a knight over it. And you are now a 'Lady. Lady Adeylia.' How does that sound?"

"It sounds fishy to me," said the mouse. "A little fly on the wall told me a different story. I just came in here to give you a piece of my mind and the rest of your scarf back. So now that you have both, I'll thank you never to talk to me again. And James, stay out of my computer chat-room as well."

James looked shocked but setbacks from women such as these don't disturb knights of the realm. They just snap their fingers, make a cutting remark, and ride away on their horses.

So James said, "That would be *Sir* James, KCB to you," and since he didn't have a horse, he just walked out of the room, catching his sword on a door latch again.

He headed straight for Mary's room and rapped politely on the door. "Mary, are you home?"

"You can't come in," came a faint reply.

"Why? I need to talk to you."

"I'm in a bubble bath."

"So?"

"So stay out until I'm finished and dressed to receive guests."

"How long will that be?"

"Not longer than three hours, I should think. Why don't you go have dinner and then come back."

"I'm not hungry."

"Right! Since when? Well, if you insist, I'll hurry. But don't come in until I'm ready. Promise?"

"I promise," said James and he sat down on the floor in the hall.

Two hours later Mary opened the door and found him asleep, nestled up to his sword. She nudged him with her foot and he scrambled to his feet, blushing profusely, she was pleased to note.

"Mer, my dear friend," he began.

"Mer?" she interrupted.

"La Mer, the sea," he said. "My new name for you because your eyes are so deep and blue."

"Mare?" she said. "I don't like it. Sounds like you're calling me a horse. And what happened to my scarf?"

"Oh Mary, that's what I'm here to tell you," said James. "A dragon-snake ate the other half. It was attacking Levancrieff Castle so I slew it. The fight lasted even longer than one of your bubble baths, but in the end my quickness and cunning prevailed over its size and flaming nostrils. I was able to finish it off with a blade to the heart, which I figured to be about six feet above its belt. Since it was so long it took over two hours to die. From head to tail. Sorry about the scarf."

"Oh James, were you injured?" gasped Mary in mock horror. She thought about confronting James with the other half of the scarf, but then decided she'd rather live with his lies than without his romantic stories and company.

"Not a scratch, just the scarf," said James. "But the best thing is, they made me a knight for saving the castle. Everybody has to call me sir, and guess what? They must now call you 'Lady. Lady Mary,' how does that sound?"

"My, that sounds great. Does Adeylia have to say it too?"

"It's the kings command! Only the lady of a knight shouldn't be so much taller than him. So you'll have to become six again."

"We've been through this before, James," said Mary. "I'd rather you become twelve. As a six-year-old I won't have the hand-span to reach all the harpsichord keys or hold a tatting shuttle properly."

James furrowed his brow, but to his knightly credit he didn't start to cry. Later, on a visit to the castle, he learned that every knight must have a lady. He kept telling them that his lady preferred to stay in the Manor, but sooner or later he knew he would be found out. Eventually he would have to give up his knighthood.

He began to think that being a pirate was a better profession, since it didn't involve girls, who were turning out to be entirely too complicated and tedious.

Late one night he tapped on Mary's door and pleaded with her to go through the secret panel with him and up the stairs to the three doors. She said no at first but when he threatened to break down, she relented. Secretly she'd been thinking that the age of six wasn't all that bad, and then she could be with James. But at age six would she even be interested in him? Well, maybe she should at least try. After all, how many men would be able to slay a dragon for her?

They had to carry candles and tiptoe all the way up to the three doors. James was in his pirate clothes, but Mary was still in her long flannel nightgown and bare feet.

"Do you know what's behind the third door?" he asked.

"No," she said. "Something new for me to learn, I suppose."

With this James opened the door, but the room was empty and dark. It smelled musty. Slowly, as things came into focus, Mary could just make out the familiar shape of Château Fantastique. Yes, it was the bats room. "How many ways are there into the bat's room?" She wondered. But he was out for a light breakfast.

"Chee. James. Mary. Oh, you two again!" he said when he finally came back.

"I need some advice," said James.

"There are many doors to knowledge, but only one to wisdom, only one that leads to salvation," said the bat.

"This girl you provided for me is too old," said James, avoiding Mary's eyes. "I'd like you to make her six."

"Even bats aren't magicians, why do you want her six?"

"She's taller and beats me in everything."

"Then why don't you become twelve?"

"I've heard that girls are smarter than boys at twelve, and I don't want her smarter than me."

"That's a bunch of hooey, and even if it were true, we can't make her do anything against her will. Besides she wasn't provided for your gratification and pleasure. She's your opposite but equal."

"Well in that case, I'd like to stay just like I am and leave this mansion now," pronounced James. "Is that possible?"

Mary glared at him, "I don't think we should leave this place yet," she said. "I'm not ready. I have so much to learn. Then we can leave."

"Actually I don't want you with me anymore," said James. "No offense, but you're just a girl. No thrill in that. I just want to go out and be a little boy again in the real world. I want to climb trees and chase squirrels. I want to get really muddy and ruin my new shoes. I want to tease people with frogs and throw rocks at spider webs. Can I do that now, Mister bat?" Mary just stared at him.

"You'll run afoul of your former self," said the bat, "unless you go through a complete and total non-recall procedure."

"What's that?" asked James.

"It means a brain reformat. You'll be a blank hard-disk so you can amalgamate with your real six-year-old self out in the actual world. You'll remember nothing of the life you are living in here, or your former life as an adult either. Are you sure you want to take this step?"

"Can I take my pirate suit?"

"You go in spirit only. The real James will suspect nothing. And you will carry nothing with you, not even your awareness. Occasionally there do occur time shift anomalies in the real world, but they are usually harmless. I've never seen one myself, but my mother speaks of them."

"Will it hurt?"

"It's like falling asleep."

"And never waking up," said Mary.

"No," said the bat, "and waking up as the real you. Only you don't realize you've been asleep. Did you know the James in real life is a sweet, quiet, well behaved boy who likes piano and parlor games most of all. I don't think any of your wild inclinations will transfer over."

"We'll see about that," said James. "So when do we start?

"James are you sure?" Mary's eyes were almost pleading. "I'll be so lonely in here. What if I become six for you? Will you stay?"

James stared her in the eye. "If I don't particularly like you at twelve, what makes you think I'd fancy you at six?"

Mary's mouth went completely dry. Her eyes narrowed and her jaw set. "I see," she said with steely eyes, and stormed out of the room and back to bed.

"So why are you still here?" said the bat to James. "Your own attitudes are all the magic you need to free yourself."

So James marched out the door of the Mansion, and then *through* the locked door of the third story room. This so startled a large rat that it bumped into a table, knocking down and breaking a teacup. "Now I've seen everything," it said, "a semi-transparent human." James glided down two staircases, and out into the yard to find James in his favorite tree. Only he wasn't there. You see he was *afraid* to climb trees. Instead he was in the kitchen helping Aunt Clara and his sister Katherine make brownies. Neither of them noticed him when he entered, even when he tried to pull Katherine's hair. James noticed his other self measuring out flour next to Katherine. "What a sissy," he reflected. "What a wus." Without further ado he sidled up to himself and gave himself a big bear hug. Then nothing. He went blank.

Well not nothing. Not blank. He dropped the cup of flour and stared up into Katherine's disapproving eyes. "Well you made me spill it," he said. "You bumped me!"

"I did not!" she protested, and turned red.

He stared at her. "Anyway, this is stupid," he barked into her face. "You *make* the cakes. I'll *eat* the cakes. Call me when they're ready. I'll be outside up a tree! And make a few jellyrolls while you're at it."

Katherine and Aunt Clara exchanged questioning glances. Suddenly they were both hit with headaches but in a few moments that had subsided. As for James, they just figured he had finally become a real boy. For better or worse. "I suppose someday he'll grow up and join the Navy," said Aunt Clara, putting her fingers to her temples. "I can almost see him in a uniform." Something felt odd but she couldn't quite put her finger on it.

Back upstairs, as Mary lay in her bed, an ever so small tear appeared in the corner of her eye and started down her cheek toward the pillow. It tickled so she wiped it away roughly and turned her face to the wall.

~26~
My Final Word

Oh my, I seem to have got carried away, and this book has gone on and on. Actually I was hardly getting started, but now I've run out of pages to write on. I only have one more after this one.

Anyway, Mary is now alone in the house. As a twelve-year-old she got trapped in it. Remember how I rescued her in the last book? Well after that, she hadn't lived very long with Aunt Clara before she got completely bored and fed up – good though the food may have been. She was essentially a teenager, for goodness sake. Aunt Clara allowed no TV, no movies, and no dating. No phone calls either. And she even home-schooled Mary, never really letting her leave the house. Most of the school stuff she had already learned in Mousumerset Manor. She wanted to get out and see the world but was allowed no further than the backyard.

Finally one day she did a very childish thing. Instead of running away into the real world, or growing up in it, she simply stole the key and set off for the third floor again. So as not to be seen, even through a window, she went all the way into the château and stayed there. Her childishness got her in, but once again, her true age wouldn't let her out. She became captive.

As time passed, even in the château, even in the treasure room full of costumes, she became bored and longed for one specific thing. Someone to play with. But not little brat James who had betrayed her. Someone her age. Someone more mature. And, wonder of wonders, she actually thought of *me*.

But no one ever came to the third floor those days. No humans anyway. Except – well there was Katherine – a grownup Katherine, with children. She visited the third floor on rare occasions, just to peer into windows and call out names like Ivanhoho, and Adeylia. Nobody paid even the slightest attention to her because she was a grownup.

Still, Mary's heart made her take a chance and wedge a note halfway out a window where Katherine would be sure to find it on her next visit. The note, in elegant, tiny handwriting, spoke cryptically:

Willy, find me at Smary@ChâteauChic.com

Endnotes:

[1] Baby shower timeline is adapted from
www.babyshowerstuff.com
[2] The Samurai Creed is adapted from
http://mcel.pacificu.edu/as/students/bushido/bcreed.html

Colossians 2:8

See to it that no one takes you **captive** through
hollow and deceptive philosophy,
which depends on human tradition and
the basic principles of this world
rather than on Christ.

The Holy Bible
New International Version

www.ingramcontent.com/pod-product-compliance
Lightning Source LLC
Chambersburg PA
CBHW032150020726
47496CB00003B/810